CONNECT THE DOTS

Keith Calabrese

Also by Keith Calabrese

A Drop of Hope

Wild Ride

CONNECT THE

DOTS

→ Keith Calabrese ←

SCHOLASTIC INC.

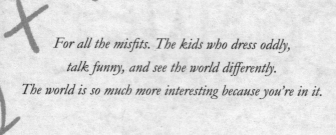

*For all the misfits. The kids who dress oddly,
talk funny, and see the world differently.
The world is so much more interesting because you're in it.*

Copyright © 2020 by Keith Calabrese

This book was originally published in hardcover by Scholastic Press in 2020.

All rights reserved. Published by Scholastic Inc., *Publishers since 1920.* SCHOLASTIC and associated logos are trademarks and/or registered trademarks of Scholastic Inc.

The publisher does not have any control over and does not assume any responsibility for author or third-party websites or their content.

No part of this publication may be reproduced, stored in a retrieval system, or transmitted in any form or by any means, electronic, mechanical, photocopying, recording, or otherwise, without written permission of the publisher. For information regarding permission, write to Scholastic Inc., Attention: Permissions Department, 557 Broadway, New York, NY 10012.

This book is a work of fiction. Names, characters, places, and incidents are either the product of the author's imagination or are used fictitiously, and any resemblance to actual persons, living or dead, business establishments, events, or locales is entirely coincidental.

ISBN 978-1-338-35404-1

10 9 8 7 6 5 4 3 2   22 23 24 25 26

Printed in the U.S.A. 40
This edition first printing 2022

Book design by Baily Crawford

PROLOGUE

TWENTY-FIVE YEARS AGO

"What if I told you that I could guarantee someone the perfect day?"

Jimmy was used to his best friend, Preston, saying weird things like this while they walked to school.

Several long seconds passed in silence.

Jimmy stopped walking. "Preston," he warned.

"Yes?"

"You're doing it again." Like many ridiculously smart people, Preston had a habit of looking past what was right in front of him, as well as abandoning conversations in mid-thought.

"Oh," Preston said, staring at Jimmy searchingly. "You'd like me to explain?"

"Sure."

The alert on Preston's digital wristwatch went off.

Beep!

Preston checked his watch. "Okay, but we need to keep moving. Kind of on a schedule here."

"What schedule?" Jimmy said, but Preston had already started walking again.

"You know when something really good happens," Preston said as Jimmy caught up to him, "and people say, 'I guess I was just in the right place at the right time'?"

"Sure."

"Well, I came up with a formula to figure out exactly when and where the right place and time would be for something really good to happen."

"Using math?"

"Yes, I thought that was implied by my use of the word 'formula.'"

"To guarantee someone a perfect day?"

"Uh-huh," Preston said. "It's really just a question of transposing a series of everyday situational elements into variables in a mathematical equation. After that, the algorithm practically writes itself."

"Oh, I'll bet," Jimmy said. He was used to this, too. To call Preston good at math wasn't just an understatement; it somehow missed the mark. Like saying a fish is good at swimming. It wasn't something Preston did, really. It was something he was.

The boys approached a yellow, two-story Shaker house. "So, who is the lucky recipient of this perfect day you've somehow calculated?"

Preston's watch went *Beep!* again just as an eleven-year-old girl came bounding out the front door to join them.

"Hey, guys!" Floss called.

"Right," Jimmy said.

"So, what do you think?" she said, doing a little twirl to show off her new skirt.

"Is that a kilt?" Jimmy asked.

"Uh-huh," Floss said. "My dad brought it back from his trip to Scotland. It's authentic Highland tartan or something."

"Did your brother get one, too?" Jimmy chuckled.

"Nah, he got bagpipes. You don't think it's too dorky, do you?" she said, suddenly a little self-conscious.

"No way. I think it looks awesome," Preston said.

Floss beamed. "Thanks, Preston."

Preston's watch went *Beep!* again.

It went on like that for the rest of the morning.

In science class, the egg Preston and Floss were incubating finally hatched a chick, right in Floss's hands.

Beep!

In math, Floss got the second-highest test grade, behind Preston.

"I'll get you next time," she said, punching Preston playfully on the shoulder.

Beep!

In gym class, they were supposed to play dodgeball, which Floss hated because it's barbaric, but the gym teacher had jury duty, so they got to do whatever they wanted to for the period.

Beep!

"Okay, how are you doing this?" Jimmy hissed over the lunch table at Preston.

"I'm not doing it, Jimmy. That's the point. I just know what's going to happen and when. Think of it like an eclipse. Astronomers use math to figure out when the sun, the moon, and the earth will all line up in a specific, exact order. Except instead of when the next eclipse is going to happen, I've solved for—"

"Tater tots!" Floss said, plopping down next to Preston with her lunch tray.

"What?" Jimmy said.

"Guys, look," she said, pointing to her tray. "The good tater tots are back! Today! I mean, imagine the odds, right?"

Beep!

Isn't it awesome? Preston mouthed across the table to Jimmy.

It was something, all right. Jimmy always knew his best friend was super smart, but this was getting a little scary. With every *Beep!* from that wristwatch, Jimmy felt a pang in his gut that told him Preston might be messing with powers he didn't understand.

After school they went to Floss's house to play Nintendo, and her brother let them try out his new bagpipes. Then Floss's mom made her special homemade lasagna, and for dessert her dad picked up Floss's favorite ice-cream bars, Farouk's Famous Fudgsicles, on his way home from work (*Beep! Beep!* and *Beep!*).

"Take those out on the porch before you get chocolate on the couch," her mom told her and the boys.

Floss brought out her portable radio, and they went onto the porch. A few minutes later, her favorite song came on and she sang along, using her ice-cream bar as a microphone.

The performance was cut short when a beat-up Chevy Nova that was driving by backfired, causing Floss to laugh in shock.

"You know," she said, looking out over the porch as the sun set brilliantly behind the trees, "this has been the perfect day."

Jimmy braced himself for the *Beep!* from Preston's watch. But it was drowned out by a loud crash down the block, followed by lots of cursing and yelling. Just as suddenly, the teenage driver of the Chevy Nova ran past Floss's house, screaming in terror.

And then things got strange.

Because a very burly, very angry man in a polka-dotted jumpsuit and clown makeup raced after the driver. The clown was moving at a pretty impressive clip, considering his oversized shoes.

Jimmy, Floss, and all the other neighbors who'd spilled out into the street watched the absurd chase with amusement. But as Floss took Preston's arm and pointed at the enraged clown, Preston just . . . shut down. His face went blank, his expression totally catatonic as his brain struggled to process this unforeseen new variable.

It took Jimmy and Floss several minutes to get him to snap out of his stupor enough to follow them off the porch to see what was going on. Floss even took the Fudgsicle stick out of Preston's gaping mouth because she was afraid he might choke on it. A tow truck had arrived and was in the process of extricating an accordion-crunched Nissan Sentra—with *Burt the Happy Clown * Parties and Group Rates* stenciled on the driver's-side door—from the front of the teenage burnout's barely dented Chevy Nova.

Preston hardly noticed.

"I think I'm gonna go," he mumbled, shuffling away from the scene.

Jimmy glanced at Floss and shrugged. "I guess I'll go, too. See you tomorrow, Floss."

Floss, confused and a bit concerned, waved goodbye, still clutching Preston's Fudgsicle stick in her fist.

Jimmy caught up to his dejected friend. "Clowns. Who'd have figured?"

"Me, ideally," Preston replied glumly.

"You're being too hard on yourself," Jimmy said.

"The numbers were sound," Preston said. "It should have worked."

"Has it occurred to you that maybe you're overthinking all of this?"

"No."

"Look, you wanted Floss to have a great day. And she did. The thing with the angry clown didn't mess that up. In fact, it was kind of hilarious."

"That's not the point," Preston said, frustrated.

"Why not?"

"Because I didn't know it was going to happen."

"So what? Who wants to know everything that's going to happen?"

"I do!"

Jimmy sighed. "Anyway, why was it so important for Floss to have a perfect day?"

"Because that was the experiment, Jimmy. Because—"

"Because you like her."

"What? No. I don't, I mean . . . So?"

"Preston, why don't you just tell her?"

"Are you serious? With no research methodology? No probability schematics?"

"I don't know what those things are. But no."

Preston considered for a long moment. "That's just insane."

"No, it's not," Jimmy said. "Whatever today was, *that* was insane. You tried to outsmart life, Preston. And it threw an angry clown at you."

Preston stopped right there on the sidewalk.

"Of course," he said quietly. Then, louder: "That's genius!" Preston grabbed Jimmy by the shoulders, a smile of inspiration plastered across his face.

"Well, thanks, I— Wait, no. No! No!"

Jimmy smacked his head in frustration while Preston started scurrying down the street.

"No," Jimmy sighed helplessly.

"It's so obvious," Preston muttered to himself. "Insert an independent variable to alter the equation."

Jimmy went after him. "Wait. What are you talking about?"

"Don't you see?" Preston said, continuing down the street. "I've been going about this all wrong. I've been solving for *when* the conditions involved in a perfect moment will simultaneously occur. Instead, I should have been working out *how* to create those conditions!" Preston said. "You said it yourself. Any random, trivial element, no matter how seemingly unconnected, can screw up even the best laid plans."

"Uh, yeah. Sure."

"Then it also stands to reason that I could isolate and harness a random, trivial element and use it to set other seemingly unconnected events in motion."

"You mean like a chain reaction?"

"Yes!"

"Okay," Jimmy said, nodding. "Or you know what you could do?"

"What?"

"None of the things you just said!"

But it was too late. As Jimmy watched Preston disappear back into his own mind, he heard his friend mutter something that would stay with Jimmy for years to come.

"Life threw me an angry clown. What's to stop me from throwing one back?"

CHAPTER ONE

What Oliver Knew * Who Doesn't Love a Good Orientation
Video * A Late Drop-Off * Getting to Know You, Getting to
Know All about You * Matilda's Curious Composition Book

- - - - - - - - - - - - - - -

PRESENT DAY

⟷

"All right, then," Frankie said, rubbing his hands together.
"Ready for the big pond, Oliver?"

Oliver Beane and his best friend, Frankie Figge, stood outside
the massive, newly refurbished building that would be their aca-
demic home for the next three years.

"No," Oliver said.

"Aw, come on." Frankie gave Oliver a nudge with his
elbow. "I say in three months you and I will be running
this place."

"Oh yeah?"

"Six tops." Frankie smirked with a cocksure confidence

that never ceased to amaze Oliver. Frankie could have been the poster child for goofy twelve-year-old awkwardness: big feet and hands; long, skinny legs and arms; and a boy's shoulders trying to hold up a man's head. Fortunately for Frankie, he had an unshakable sense of self-esteem. He wasn't full of himself, exactly. He just liked who he was and seemed to figure that everyone else would eventually catch on, sooner or later.

Despite his best friend's back-to-school spirit, Oliver was not feeling the middle school love. About a year ago, Oliver's parents had gotten a divorce after his father left them for a twenty-eight-year-old Pilates instructor named Selene. Then, a few months ago, his father and Selene moved to Phoenix. Oliver knew that starting middle school was supposed to be a big deal, a major life event. But as far as he was concerned, he'd had enough major life events for a while.

Frankie and Oliver made their way up the steps to the main doors, where Oliver collided briefly with a surly, hulking boy.

"Watch it, turdburger," the boy growled as he elbowed Oliver aside and went into the school.

"Okay, maybe it'll take eight months," Frankie said as they stepped into the school.

Eight months. The truth was that Oliver doubted he'd still be around in eight months. A few weeks ago, Oliver's uncle Tommy, his mother's older brother, had driven all the way from Massachusetts to visit for a few days. His mom and Uncle Tommy were close, and Oliver knew that his uncle was pressing for her and Oliver to move to Belchertown, where he owned a chain of tire stores. Oliver knew this because while Uncle Tommy was staying with them, he kept dropping subtle hints about how great Belchertown was, how much there was to do, how much fun Oliver would have.

It didn't take a genius to put it together.

Oliver and his mom lived in the town of Lake Grove Glen, about thirty miles west by northwest of Chicago, in the house where his mom grew up. He'd always liked Lake Grove Glen— it had a way of being small-town and a little bit city at the same time, and he didn't want to leave. But ever since things had started changing, it didn't feel like his hometown anymore. Lately, it just felt like another part of his life that, soon, wouldn't be.

As Oliver and Frankie made their way into the auditorium for orientation, Oliver bumped into the school janitor, a thin, wiry, and very shaggy man.

"Oh, sorry, sir," Oliver said.

The janitor mumbled something back and scurried away.

"Man, twice in one day," Frankie chided Oliver. "It's like you're not even here, buddy."

"Who, you may ask, is Preston Oglethorpe?" the narrator intoned rhetorically. "Only the smartest man you've probably never heard of!"

Oliver, Frankie, and the rest of the sixth-grade class were crammed into the school auditorium for a morning orientation, the culmination of which was an informational video, projected on a massive whiteboard screen up on the stage. The video was shot in the retro-throwback style of those old 1950s educational films with all the random pops and scratches of old film stock.

A file photo of an adult Preston Oglethorpe, staring blankly at the camera in an awkwardly fitting suit and tie, was replaced on the screen by one of a younger Preston Oglethorpe winning a school science fair.

"A former student at this very school, Preston won the state science fair in sixth grade but then left our hallowed halls in seventh grade . . . for MIT!"

A series of photos followed showing Preston Oglethorpe in college, head and shoulders below all the other kids in his classes.

"Preston went on to graduate at the ripe old age of fourteen and earned the first of several PhDs, this one in applied mathematics, by the time he turned seventeen. Then, at twenty-eight,

Preston won the Nobel Prize in Physics for his work in applied chaos theory."

Oliver couldn't stop thinking about the faraway look in the man's eyes. Oliver knew he was supposed to be impressed, but despite all the glamorous pictures of Preston Oglethorpe winning awards and meeting powerful and famous people, Oliver just felt sad for the guy. He never looked happy; he never even smiled.

"But then," the narrator continued as the music took on an ominous tone, "Preston Oglethorpe suddenly *vanished*. To this day, no one knows where he went or even if he is still alive."

The screen dissolved into a huge, cheesy question mark superimposed over a portrait shot of Preston Oglethorpe.

"So where is Preston Oglethorpe now? Well, that is one mystery which, truly, only he can solve."

The lights came up and the kids were dismissed to their classes.

"Neat video, eh?" Frankie said as they were walking back to class. "Kind of bogus, though, how the first thing we learn here is about a guy who already makes our lives seem small and meaningless by comparison. I mean, like sixth grade isn't intimidating enough without reminding us that we're totally basic?"

Oliver wasn't really listening. He was still thinking about Preston Oglethorpe and that faraway, lonely look in his eyes.

Matilda Sandoval and her dad sat in the car outside school. All the other kids were inside; the school day was already underway. It was a routine of sorts. Showing up a little late, when everyone was in class, made being the new kid, if not easier, at least less hectic.

This wasn't the first time they had done this. Matilda doubted it would be the last.

"You know," her dad said, "I had to start at a new school when I was about your age."

He'd never said that any of the other times. Matilda wondered if he'd been saving it.

"Across the street," Matilda said as she opened the worn composition book resting on her lap. "Four o'clock. Little warm for such a heavy coat. Possible shoplifter, maybe a concealed weapon."

Her dad followed her gaze as she jotted down her observations in the composition book. He spotted the suspect, a little old lady in a winter coat, as she entered a dry cleaner.

"Ummm, okay," her dad said. "I'll look into it."

Matilda finished writing, snapped the composition book closed, and got out of the car.

"Don't forget your physical therapy," she said, poking her head back in.

"I won't," her father said with a wistful smile. "Have a good day, okay?"

Matilda nodded soberly, shut the door, and headed into the school.

Oliver's first impression of the new girl was that she was the most serious person he'd ever seen in his entire life. Her posture was right out of a health book, her stride quick and all business. Even her hair was intense, tightly coiled in a ponytail that tolerated no dissension in the ranks.

The principal had brought her into the classroom at the start of the period, but somehow it seemed like he was following her into the room.

"Good morning, Mr. Pembleton," Principal Wilson said to their teacher while the serious girl stood at the front of the room, sizing things up. "Sorry to interrupt," he continued. "But I have a new student for you. This is Matilda San—"

"If I may, Principal Wilson," the girl said, stepping forward to address the class. "Good morning, my name is Matilda Sandoval. I like to be called Matty, but, well, no one ever does."

Mr. Pembleton and Principal Wilson looked at each other quizzically, unsure whether or not one of them should reclaim the floor, so to speak.

"I've lived in four different cities in the last three years," the new girl, Matilda, continued. "For any mathletes in the room, that's a new school roughly every two hundred and seventy-three days."

Oliver caught her giving a slight nod to two boys in the back who were presently checking her long division.

"My passions are modern surveillance techniques and staying current on the latest advances in computer encryption. I also enjoy true crime novels, play a passable flute, and am dreadful at any sport involving a ball."

She then turned her attention to the teacher. "Mr. Pembleton, shall I take that empty desk by the window?"

"Pardon? Who?" Mr. Pembleton stumbled, caught off guard at suddenly having his class returned to him. "Oh, yes. That will be fine, Matilda."

After Matilda passed Oliver on her way to the desk she essentially assigned to herself, Frankie leaned over to him. "Well, that was different."

"Yeah," Oliver said absently as he watched the new girl take her seat. She sat up straight in her chair, folded her hands, and looked dead ahead as Mr. Pembleton resumed class. But her shoulders sagged a bit, and Oliver sensed that even though it was still just the morning, she'd already had a long day.

"Hey, Oliver. How old do you have to be to trade penny stocks?" Frankie asked, reading a pop-up ad on his phone.

It was lunchtime. The boys sat at the end of a long cafeteria table, by themselves.

"I'm guessing thirteen, at least," Oliver said. "Still pushing for that dog?"

"Uh-huh," Frankie said, putting his phone down on the table. "But between the twins acting like little maniacs and my dad starting his new catering business, it's 'not a good time,' which is parent-speak for—"

"Not enough money," Oliver said, finishing the thought.

At the other end of the long table, a big kid in a Clash T-shirt and Doc Martens walked over and knocked a lunch tray to the floor. Oliver recognized him as the kid he'd collided with on the way into school this morning.

"That's Billy Fargus," Frankie said. "A girl in homeroom was telling me about him."

"What's his deal?"

"Lunches," Frankie said. "He has a thing for eating ones that belong to other people."

"Great."

"Yeah. Apparently, he picks on a different kid each day. So I guess the good news is you only have to give up your lunch once and then you're done."

Oliver and Frankie watched as Billy Fargus reached across the table and proceeded to rifle through another student's food. When the kid started to protest, Billy leaned over and whispered something in his ear. The kid's eyes got big and he gave up the sandwich.

Oliver and Frankie shared a look.

"Then again," Frankie said, "I imagine the anticipation will get stressful."

"Hi there. May I sit?" It was the girl from earlier that morning, and she'd already plopped down at the table. "Oliver and . . . Frankie, right?"

"Yeah," Frankie said guardedly. "How did you—"

"Hi," Oliver said, a step behind.

Matilda plowed ahead. "So, like I mentioned earlier, I move around a lot. As such, I like to cut to the chase, making-friends-wise."

Oliver was still confused but kind of charmed at the same time. Frankie, less so.

"And you've, what?" Frankie said. "Settled on us?"

"Well," Matilda said, giving Frankie a quick once-over, "judging by your clothes, you're clearly not hung up on labels or social status, which suggests a more accepting, nonconformist personality."

Frankie looked at Oliver. "Did she just take a shot?"

"Wow," Oliver said. "That was really good."

Frankie, unimpressed, started digging through his lunch.

"Thanks," Matilda said, turning her attention to him. "Now, you." She took a moment or two appraising Oliver. "Your body language, posture, and overall withdrawn bearing suggest a recently dissolved family unit. Within the last year, for sure. And by the looks of your well-balanced lunch, I'm guessing Dad did the actual, physical separating?"

Oliver looked away, stung.

"Hey," Frankie cut in. "Back off!"

Matilda blinked in surprise, like someone who'd been caught daydreaming.

"It's okay, Frankie," Oliver said.

"No, it's not," Matilda said, crestfallen, as she looked down and wrung her hands anxiously. "I'm sorry, Oliver. I don't mean anything by it. I just . . . I should go."

She was up and off before Oliver could gather himself to stop her. On her way out of the cafeteria, Oliver watched her sidestep the shaggy janitor Oliver had bumped into earlier, who was now cleaning up the downed lunch tray.

Matilda gave the boys a wide berth the rest of the day. Oliver felt bad and nearly convinced himself to go up and talk to her, just to tell her no hard feelings and all that. But pretty much everything about her intimidated him, and he feared what other unflattering truth bombs she might uncover from the way he walked or his speech patterns.

He saw her again after school, sitting by a tree on the front lawn and scribbling furiously in a black composition book.

Oliver gave Frankie a nudge. "I wonder what she's writing," he said.

"I don't," Frankie said. "The girl's strange." He looked down self-consciously at his shirt. "I mean, this works, right?"

As the boys started walking home, Oliver stole one last glance at Matilda, who was still under the tree, writing.

Frankie's house was first, but when they reached the drive, Frankie just stood there, stalling.

"What are you doing?"

"I don't want to go in," Frankie said, as if they were staring at Frankenstein's castle and not a two-story Craftsman on one of the least ominous blocks in northern Illinois.

"C'mon," Oliver said.

"I'm serious, man," Frankie said. "It's chaos in there. We're talking *Lord of the Files*, pre-K edition. I actually prefer school. The quiet . . ."

At his house, Oliver always saw quiet as the enemy. It wasn't peaceful or contemplative. Quiet was words never said. Quiet was lonely.

When Oliver's parents got divorced, his father had said that they'd still be a family. That was a lie. When his dad said he was moving to Phoenix, he'd insisted that he would still be a big part of Oliver's life. That was an even bigger lie.

Oliver's mom had lied, too. But those lies were different. When his dad moved out, she hadn't said it was because he was small and selfish and twenty-eight-year-old fitness instructors don't come along every day. She'd said sometimes people grow apart.

That's when things had started getting quiet.

The front door burst open and Frankie's dad leaned halfway out. He wore a chef's apron covered in sauce and had a very frazzled expression on his face.

"Frankie, great! You're home," he said with a heavy sigh of relief. "I really need some help in here. Mom's still at the lab, the twins just threw up on each other, and I've got three burners going."

Frankie gave Oliver a look. "See what I mean?"

"Oh, hey there, Oliver!" Frankie's dad said. "Tell your mom

not to cook tonight. Once Elaine gets home from work, I'm sending her over with a new primavera I've been working on."

"Okay," said Oliver. "Thanks, Mr. Figge."

Oliver suddenly felt very tired as he continued on to his own house. It had been a long day, and a strange one, too. Between that weird orientation video, a menacing (though, to be fair, equal opportunity) sandwich bully, and a strange girl who could tell everything about him by the contents of his lunch and the way he sat in a chair, middle school sure wasn't shaping up like he'd expected.

CHAPTER TWO

The Flying Figge Brothers * Matilda Finishes Unpacking *
I Didn't Realize This Was a Party Line * A Not So Private
Conversation * Tears of a Sullivan * That's Certainly One
Way to Make Friends

Frankie sat on his bed staring out the window as he briefly contemplated climbing through it and living a life on the run. There wasn't any big dramatic reason for this train of thought. He hadn't gotten in trouble with the law or school, and he hadn't just had a blowout fight with his parents. The reason Frankie imagined running away was, in fact, not a very compelling one:

His mother had left to bring food over to Oliver and his mom.

Which meant that his dad was alone downstairs with the twins. And any minute now, he'd be needing help.

Frankie didn't want to help.

It was chaos downstairs. Bedlam. Anarchy. And so noisy.

Frankie's twin brothers, Seamus and Hugh, were a little under two years old, but already they were totally out of control. He'd never seen them walk—they went directly from a rodent-like, scampering crawl to constant, maniacal running. The only time they ever stopped was when they collided into something heavier than they were, like a wall or the couch or Frankie. They climbed on everything, touched everything, broke everything. They were impossible to contain, and no amount of baby-proofing would ever be sufficient to protect them or the house. While you tried to stop one of them from removing the cover to the light socket, the other would be trying to play red rover against the ottoman.

And they never left him alone. Their two favorite words were "Frankie" and "watch." For example, one of them, probably Hugh, would yell, "Frankie!" Seamus would answer with, "Frankie, FRANKIE!" Then, together, they'd howl, "FRANKIE, WATCH!!" and start hurling couch pillows at the ceiling fan.

Still, at least they acknowledged him. If his parents didn't need him for something, they barely even registered Frankie's presence anymore, though he honestly couldn't blame them. Their hands were too full with his berserk brothers to even think to stop and ask him how his day had been. He accepted that they were doing what they had to do to survive.

Frankie heard a scream downstairs, followed immediately by a crash. Or maybe it had been a crash, followed immediately by a scream. It was hard to tell anymore.

Three, two, one, Frankie thought.

"Hey, Frankie!" he heard his dad call up the stairwell. "Think you could come down here and give me a hand?"

Matilda's mom had picked up the ingredients for make-your-own-pizzas for dinner. Matilda used to love pizza, but not anymore.

Matilda remembered reading once about conditioned response. It was like that experiment with the dogs, where the guy would ring a bell right before he fed them. After a while, the dogs knew that the bell meant food, and their mouths would water before the food was even brought out.

The thing about a conditioned response, though, was that it could work the other way, too.

Whenever Matilda's dad would get a new assignment and they'd have to suddenly pack up and move to some new city, he would bring home pizza, with all her favorite toppings, to help break the news. This most recent move had been the hardest yet. About eight months ago, her dad had been promoted to a desk job and transferred to Washington, DC. It was the best of both worlds for the Sandovals. They could finally put down some roots, and even more importantly for Matilda, it meant her dad was finally out of the field.

Then, six weeks ago, her dad brought home pizza, and . . . Hello, Lake Grove Glen.

Now whenever Matilda saw pizza, it had the opposite effect that it did on those drooling dogs. Pizza made her think about moving again, starting over again, not knowing anyone again.

Pizza made her stomach drop.

She picked at her slice for a while, hoping her parents wouldn't realize that she hadn't eaten much of it, and then went upstairs to finish unpacking.

Matilda usually unpacked and set up her new room immediately, but this time she found herself dragging it out. She didn't hold on to much, just the barest essentials. Other than her clothes, all she had was her computer, one picture of her and her parents on vacation in Canada (before Dayton and, well, before), and some books, most of which were nonfiction and highly technical.

Her walls were mostly bare except for two posters, one of a popular boy band and the other a movie poster from *Moonglow*, a teen supernatural romance franchise that was apparently all the rage with girls her age. Matilda had zero interest in the content behind either of these posters but displayed them in the hopes of tricking her parents into believing that she had some "normal" interests. She didn't want them to worry about her being weird. Well, *too* weird, at any rate.

Matilda took the last book out of the last cardboard box and put it on the bookcase, an action that might have felt significant if she hadn't done it so many times in the last couple of years.

Then she went back downstairs to say good night to her parents. They were in the living room, watching television. Her mom sat on the couch while her dad was parked on the floor in front of her. He had his left arm up halfway, like he was resting it on a car door, while Matilda's mom, holding his elbow, gently rotated his shoulder, first clockwise and then counterclockwise.

Her father wore a sleeveless workout shirt, one that obscured but didn't completely cover the circular scar on his chest, just below the collarbone. The one from a bullet that missed his heart by an inch and a half. In movies when the hero gets shot, it's always conveniently "in and out," but her dad's bullet wasn't one of those. It bounced around inside him, breaking his scapula and his collarbone before resting in his deltoid muscle until an ER doctor yanked it out.

Dayton.

"Hey, sweetie," her mom said as her dad subtly fixed the shirt to hide his scar. "Come join us."

Matilda's dad got off the floor, and three of them sat on the couch and watched television. Then her mom got up to make some tea.

"I have to go out of town next week," her dad said when it was just the two of them. "Work trip."

"Okay," Matilda said. "How long?"

"Three days, two nights," he said. "I should be back for dinner on Thursday."

"Flying or driving?"

"Driving."

They did this whenever Matilda's dad had to travel, which was a lot. He wasn't allowed to talk about his work much, so they came up with this game to make up for it. Matilda got five questions, which he could decline to answer if he had to, but under no circumstances was he allowed to lie.

"So it's not far, then," Matilda surmised. "In state?"

"Out of state."

Matilda bit her lip. "Will you be changing time zones?"

Her dad didn't answer right away.

"Well?"

"I'm thinking," he said defensively. "Yes."

"Interesting," Matilda said, staring intently at her father's eyes.

"Are you looking for micro-expressions?"

"Yes."

"Stop it," he laughed.

"No," she said. "It's fair game."

"Fine," he conceded. "You have one left."

"Got it. Your destination—is the population over or under two hundred thousand residents?"

"Over."

"Okay," she said, satisfied.

Matilda gave her dad a hug and a kiss good night and went up to change and brush her teeth. It was weird playing the game with her dad now. Before it was just a goof, so when she couldn't figure out where he was going, it didn't really matter. But since he got shot . . .

At least she knew he wasn't going back to Dayton; it had a population of roughly one hundred and forty thousand people.

Matilda climbed into bed but wasn't ready to go to sleep yet. Seeing her dad's scar and playing their old game was sending her thoughts where she didn't want them to go. Deep down she just knew that this move to Lake Grove Glen meant that her dad was back in the field.

Of course, once she let the thought in her head, she couldn't shake it. She considered getting out her laptop when her mom poked her head in the door.

"Knock, knock," her mom said, coming in and taking a seat at the foot of Matilda's bed.

"Tucking me in?" Matilda said.

"I could if you'd like."

"That's all right."

"Tell you a bedtime story?" her mom pressed. "Or, hey, you could tell me one."

"Okay," Matilda said. "There once was a little girl who traveled the world with her wonderful parents. And even though they moved around a lot and none of the places they went were ever very interesting, the little girl was still very happy because she was loved so very much, and in the end that's all that ever really matters. The end."

Matilda's mom looked at her in a hard to read way. Then she said, "Kinda asked for that, didn't I?"

"I'm okay, Mom," Matilda said. "Really."

Matilda's mom kissed her on the forehead. "I know you are," she said, getting up from the bed. On the way out she did a double take at the posters Matilda had hung.

"*Moonglow*, huh?" her mom said.

"Well, it's no *Big Trouble in Little China*," Matilda said.

It was a little family joke. *Big Trouble in Little China* was her dad's favorite movie of all time. He had a framed poster of it hanging in his office and a collector's coffee mug as well. Matilda had watched it with him once, on her computer while he was recuperating in the hospital. Even though the plot was a little over the top in her opinion, she'd pretended to like it because her dad had been shot and almost killed and they both just needed to feel like everything was okay again.

"Okay," her mom said. For a second, she looked like she was going to say something else. But she didn't.

Upstairs in his bedroom, Oliver was video chatting with Frankie about his suspected move.

"Belchertown?" Frankie exclaimed. "Is that even a real city?"

"In Massachusetts."

"C'mon, it has to be a made-up place. Like Timbuktu or Walla Walla."

"Those are real places, too, Frankie."

Oliver hadn't meant to get into it, because saying it out loud made it seem all the more inevitable. But Frankie didn't miss much, and when he asked Oliver why he'd been acting all quiet and moody lately, Oliver finally told him.

"Dang," Frankie said. "This really blows."

Matilda Sandoval's face popped up on the screen. "What blows?" she asked nonchalantly.

"Whoa! Where the heck did you come from?"

It was a fair question, seeing as how a girl they had only

met this morning had now, somehow, just joined their video chat.

"You look down, Oliver," Matilda said, leaning in closer to her screen to get a better look at him.

"I think my mom and I might have to sell the house and move to Belchertown, Massachusetts, and live with my uncle."

"Seriously," Frankie said. "Did she just hack into our video chat?"

"I'm sorry, Oliver," Matilda said. "Though if it makes you feel any better, Belchertown does have a very low crime rate. Mostly petty burglary, some insurance fraud."

"Thanks, Matilda," Oliver said.

"No problem," Matilda said. "And, um, I'm sorry about lunch today."

"It's okay," Oliver said. "We're cool."

"Yeah?" Matilda said, smiling for, Oliver realized, the first time since he'd met her. "Thanks. See you tomorrow."

She disconnected, vanishing just as quickly as she'd appeared.

"Man, I'm telling you," Frankie said. "That girl is weird."

Oliver didn't see it that way, though. She was odd, there was no way around that. But the way she introduced herself in class and how she came up to them at lunch, that took nerve. It had to be tough, moving all the time, always being new. What was really weird was how she hadn't given up and become that quiet kid who disappears in the back row and does their best to stay invisible.

Weird, and also impressive.

Mrs. Figge left around eight thirty, and Oliver went downstairs to ask his mom if she needed help cleaning up.

"You're sweet," she said. "But there's not much. I've got it. So, how was your first day?"

"Okay," Oliver said. "We saw a video on that Oglethorpe guy. The one they renamed the school after."

"Oh yeah?" his mom said. "I actually grew up with him, you know."

"Really?"

His mom nodded. "We used to walk to school together."

"Wow," Oliver said. "He was really smart, huh?"

"Oh yeah."

"Kind of felt bad for him, though," Oliver ventured. "Even when he was winning all those awards and everything, he still looked sad."

Oliver's mom thought about this for a moment. "Well," she said wistfully, "Preston always had an easier time with numbers than he did with people."

"Miss anything?" the big man said as he emerged from the kitchen with a heaping mug of hot cocoa.

"Nah, just saying good night to the kid," said the other man, who was sitting at the dining room table and listening in on a black headset.

It was a strange scene. The two men were lying low in a cute little bungalow house in a neighborhood only a couple of miles away from Oliver's. But there was nothing cute about all the high-tech computer equipment on the table or the lack of serious furniture. There wasn't anything that could be considered "décor," suggesting that the house was being used less as a home and more as some kind of command center or lair.

Sullivan, the man with the cocoa, was massively built with an open, almost friendly face. He was the kind of guy people call a "big teddy bear."

Of course, people tend to forget that technically a teddy bear is still a bear.

The man listening on the headset was Gilbert. A sour, imposing man with beady eyes and a compulsive need to constantly squeeze his purple tension ball, Gilbert was, more by default than merit, the brains of the pair.

Sullivan sat down next to Gilbert and put on his headset as well. "She told him about Massachusetts yet?" he asked, a curious little tremble in his voice.

Gilbert waved his hand dismissively as they listened in on Oliver and his mom. "Shut up," he said. "They're talking about Oglethorpe." Gilbert listened some more, then picked up his cell phone and started texting.

"The boss is gonna want to hear about this," Gilbert said. "Pronto."

Sullivan wiped his nose with one sleeve, his moistened eyes with the other.

Gilbert finished his text and looked over at Sullivan. "Oh, come on," he said with disgust. "Are you . . . are you crying?"

"It's just not fair!" Sullivan bellowed now that he was outed and there was no point in hiding his emotions. "She's going to lose the house. She grew up in that house, you know."

"Geez, Sully . . ."

"She's a good mom," Sullivan whimpered. "She deserves better."

Gilbert reached over and smacked his partner upside the head. "What am I always telling you, huh?"

"Don't connect with the mark," Sullivan said, chastened.

"That's right."

Sullivan nodded in shame. Then he considered for a moment. "But, Gilbert?"

"What?"

"She's not the mark. She's the bait, right?"

"Sully."

"Uh-huh?"

"Shut up."

The shaggy janitor was still getting used to the new job. He finished at the school right around seven, at which time he got into an old Oldsmobile Cutlass and drove to several nearby supermarkets, making the exact same purchase at each one. After he finished his shopping, he came home for the night sometime around nine o'clock.

Home, curiously, was not a house or an apartment, but an old, seemingly empty brick building in the warehouse district.

Once he finished bringing all his bags of groceries inside, the shaggy janitor immediately took off his false hair, placing the wig and fake beard on a small workbench by the door. It was always the first thing he did once he no longer needed the disguise; all that bogus hair really, really itched.

In reality, the janitor was clean-shaven with short-cropped hair, a look he adopted more for its simplicity than its style.

After scratching his scalp and rubbing the feeling back into his cheeks, he finally turned on some lights.

Like the beard and wig, the old brick warehouse was itself a disguise. What looked like a run-down old building on the outside was, on the inside, a high-tech command center that would put most spy movies to shame. In addition to a slew of next-generation computer equipment, a dozen video screens hung from the ceiling showing twenty-four-hour news networks, internet feeds, and satellite imagery. Several old-school portable blackboards filled the perimeter of the space, creating a massive semicircle. At the center of the semicircle was a small living area, consisting of a refrigerator, sofa bed, table and chair, Eames recliner, and a make-shift kitchen counter piled with cheap dishware and a microwave.

The table was round and had a chair at one end and four poster-sized digital screens hanging where the other chairs should have been. Each screen displayed a portrait, three men and one woman.

"You're home later than usual," a woman's voice said as the janitor dropped the last of the grocery bags on the table. He looked up as the woman in the portrait came to life. The image was shockingly convincing, the detail so perfect it was all but impossible for the casual observer to really be sure there wasn't an actual, living person inside that picture frame.

She was a very serious-looking woman. Though she scowled frequently, her eyes were kind, albeit troubled. She wore a prim dress with a high neckline and kept her hair in a tight, efficient bun.

"Oh," he said. "Good evening, Marie."

Marie Curie frowned. "We're worried about you, Preston."

The janitor, a grown-up Preston Oglethorpe, gave Marie Curie a wry look.

"Okay, maybe not all of us," she conceded. "But I am, deeply."

"I'm fine, Marie."

"I don't think you are."

"Ach, lay off the boy, Marie," Albert Einstein said, his portrait popping awake to join the discussion. His snow-white hair leaped out in all directions, in contrast to the thick, bushy hedgehog of a mustache planted on his upper lip. The expression on his face was a mixture of weary correction and incorrigible mischief, like an uncle who always tells you that you're doing it wrong but knows all the best inappropriate jokes.

"Preston, you're home," joined in Leonardo da Vinci. "How's the new job, my boy?"

"Yes," Albert said snidely. "How goes the toilet scrubbing?"

"I wouldn't think a patent clerk would put on such airs," Leonardo quipped. He had long, flowing hair and a beard down to his chest. He looked like a wizard from a fantasy novel, except instead of the pointy hat, he wore a floppy cap that rested rather jauntily on the top of his head.

"Well, seeing as the patent clerk solved the equation of the universe—"

"What about the equation of hair care? Going to get around to that one anytime soon?"

"Will you two knock it off?" Marie interjected.

"Locks of love over there started it," Albert huffed.

Preston looked at the last portrait, the one of his fourth and final idol, Nikola Tesla. Impeccably dressed, meticulously groomed, and broodingly handsome, he had a penetrating stare that was equal parts sadness, madness, and haunted genius. Unlike the other three, his image remained frozen in portraiture, as it always was.

When Preston had first created the portraits, he spent weeks tinkering with Tesla's artificial intelligence, convinced there must be something wrong with the programming or the circuitry. But from a diagnostic point of view, everything was working as it was supposed to. Tesla just didn't want to talk.

Preston walked over to the far end of the warehouse, where he pressed a button on the wall, causing a massive dry-erase board to descend from the rafters. The whiteboard was almost as big as the wall itself, and on it was a flowchart. Starting all the way on the left side was a box with arrows coming out of it, connecting it to other boxes. Then those boxes had arrows coming out of them as well. It just kept going on like that, one box leading to another box, then another, all the way across this giant dry-erase board. And for each box there was a piece of data written inside. Sometimes the data was an event, sometimes it was a date, sometimes it was information only Preston could understand.

"Stop giving me the look, Marie," Preston said as he stared at the flowchart. She hung behind him now. Preston had hooked up his four heroes to a rack-and-pulley system that gave their screens free run of the warehouse.

"Preston, I'm begging you one last time," Marie said. "Go to the police."

"The police," Albert scoffed. "Bah! They'd be out of their league."

"It pains me, Marie, but I agree with Albert," Leonardo said. "I think we're well beyond the reach of conventional law enforcement."

"We have to do something—"

"I *am* doing something," Preston said, staring fixedly at the wall.

"Relax, Marie," Albert said drolly. "I'm sure *Flowers for Algernon* here has it all covered."

"When Townsend—"

"Don't!" Preston said quickly. "You know the rules."

"Fine." Marie sighed, rolling her eyes a little. "When *he* gets here, it won't be a laughing matter, I promise you that."

"Oh, he's here already."

The room got quiet.

"What?" Marie said softly.

"If my calculations are correct, he's already in town," Preston said patiently. "And my calculations are always correct."

"They weren't in Dayton," Albert said under his breath.

"Ouch," Leonardo said.

"Dayton was an anomaly," Preston said testily. "A fluke. I was compromised and distracted."

"Oh, and you aren't now?" Marie countered.

"For the last time," Preston said even more testily. "I know what I'm doing!"

"Very well, my dear boy," Leonardo said calmly. "But, if I may ask, what, exactly, *are* you doing? And what's in all those grocery bags?"

Preston turned around to look at the portraits.

"Cardamom," Preston said.

"Cardamom?" Albert said. "What the—"

"It's a spice," Leonardo said helpfully. "Member of the ginger family, native to India . . ."

"Oh, shut up. I know what cardamom is. But why is this idiot hoarding it?"

"Because under the right circumstances," Preston said, a slightly ominous tone creeping into his voice, "one jar of cardamom can change everything."

CHAPTER THREE

Missing Matilda ＊ Henry's Market (over on MacDonald) ＊ Billy
Fargus Can't Feel His Face ＊ Principal Wilson Opts for
Rehabilitation ＊ Matilda Returns with Bad News

Oliver spent the next week and a half trying not to think about
moving to Massachusetts. During the school day, at least, he had
plenty of distractions. Middle school was a big adjustment—
lockers, changing classes, and Billy Fargus slowly but surely making his way closer to Oliver and Frankie's end of the cafeteria table.

"What's with you?" Frankie asked.

"What?" Oliver said, looking up absently.

"You haven't even touched your lunch. What gives?"

"Matilda isn't at school today."

"So?"

Oliver shrugged. Ever since she'd hacked into Oliver and
Frankie's video chat last week, Matilda had been keeping to

herself. She'd say hello to the boys now and then, but she spent most of her free time with her nose buried in her composition book. Especially after school, when she sat under her tree and watched everyone leave, all the while writing furiously in that book.

Though Oliver was curious to find out what Matilda was writing, he was also curious about her. She'd moved around a lot, had to start over at a new school a lot, and as the prospect of moving to a new town and a new school loomed large in his near future, he was interested in what that had been like, not to mention sympathetic.

Oliver was so lost in thought that he hadn't noticed a shadow descending over him and Frankie.

"Here's the deal," the shadow, a.k.a. Billy Fargus, said, leaning across the table and staring at Frankie. "Give me your lunch and you don't eat today, or I punch you in the mouth and you don't eat for a week."

Frankie mulled it over for about a second and a half, long enough to preserve at least a modicum of dignity, and then handed over his sandwich.

"He does make a compelling argument," Frankie said as Billy Fargus walked away with his lunch.

Oliver took a bite of his own sandwich, then opened it up to look inside. "We should have given him mine," he said, slumping in his seat. "My mom forgot to buy jelly last night."

Frankie picked listlessly at Oliver's chips while watching Billy Fargus savor the gourmet sandwich Frankie's dad had made for him. The kid couldn't get enough of it, closing his eyes in delight as he crammed every last morsel into his mouth.

"Chicken pesto on olive loaf," Frankie said. "That ain't right."

"No! No, no, no!" Frankie's dad wailed from the kitchen as Oliver and Frankie entered the house.

Frankie was unfazed by his father's cries of distress. "Hey, I'm home," he called as he calmly led Oliver into the kitchen.

"Oh, hey, guys," Frankie's dad said, hanging up the phone. "Listen, I need a huge favor. I'm all out of cardamom, and the only place that has any is Henry's Market over on MacDonald, and I can't go because I have canapés in the oven for the Carmichael party."

"Fine," Frankie said, heading back to the front door.

"Thanks, buddy!" his dad called after them.

"Yeah, yeah," Frankie muttered. And like that, he and Oliver left as quickly as they'd come.

Henry's Market was a little mom-and-pop grocery store about

a twenty-minute walk from Frankie's house. Frankie stalked with a quick, irritated stride all the way to the market; Oliver had a hard time keeping up.

"Come on," Frankie said impatiently. He was already at the counter with the cardamom. "Just pick one."

Oliver stood in the jelly aisle trying to make a decision, but it wasn't going well. Usually buying jelly was not a challenging undertaking, but the aisle was full of exotic artisan jams. He just wanted basic grape or strawberry—he'd even take blackberry in a pinch—but no dice.

"All they've got are these weird flavors," Oliver said.

"Well, it's either that or another dry sandwich tomorrow."

Oliver scowled and reconsidered the selection. He settled on mango-chutney jam and joined Frankie at the counter.

The countergirl rang them up with an exhaustive sigh.

"Here," she said, pulling a piece of beef jerky from a jar on the counter and handing it to Oliver. "It comes free with the jam," she said. "It's, like, promotional."

Oliver looked quizzically at the jerky.

"Can I have it?" Frankie asked.

"You don't even like jerky," Oliver said, handing the stick of dried meat to his friend.

"I know," Frankie said, sticking it in his backpack. "But, hey, it's free."

Matilda wasn't at school again the next day. Though she was probably just sick or something, Oliver couldn't help but wonder if she'd left. For another school, another city. She did say she moved around a lot.

Her absence distracted Oliver for the entire morning and into lunch. So much so that he almost overlooked the fact that, since Billy Fargus had pillaged Frankie's lunch yesterday, it'd be his turn today.

Oliver handed over the sandwich before Billy Fargus could deliver his eat-for-a-day/eat-for-a-week spiel. (The worst sarcasm in the world is sarcasm from a bully. That's because it implies that they're getting their way through actual cleverness and not just dumb, brute force.) Oliver didn't even look at Billy, just held the bag up for him to snatch without so much as a word.

"Wow," said Frankie. "That was kind of hard-core."

Oliver shrugged. He wasn't even that hungry. Besides, he'd had to use that weird jam he'd bought yesterday. Billy Fargus was probably doing him a favor.

"Man," Frankie said. "He's really going to town on your sandwich."

Oliver turned to see that Billy wasn't so much eating Oliver's sandwich as he was flat-out inhaling it. Apparently, it tasted so good he couldn't eat it fast enough.

Then, strangely, Billy stopped chewing. He dropped the sandwich and inexplicably started slapping the sides of his face with his hands.

"Wha . . . wha . . ." Billy garbled, shaking his head frantically.

"What's he doing?" Oliver said, concerned.

"I don't know." Frankie shrugged. "But it's awesome."

"I can't feel my fwace!" Billy bellowed, his cheeks turning red from a likely combination of an allergic reaction and all the desperate slapping and shaking. He was panicking now, pinching and pulling at his ears, nose, and lips. "Iiiii cwannnn'ttt tawwwlk . . . Nooow mwyy wwips dwon't dwork!!"

"What the what?!" Frankie said as he and Oliver rushed over to Billy, who was now curled up in a whimpering ball under the table.

"Help!" Oliver called out. "Um . . . Somebody! We need help here—"

"Now, now, hold on," Frankie interrupted, staring down at the blubbering Billy Fargus. "Let's just respect the moment."

"Dude!" Oliver turned sharply to glare at his friend. "I think this is serious."

"Fine." Frankie scowled and hopped up on a chair to flag down an adult.

Billy Fargus and his mother showed up at the school office the next day to discuss Billy's lunchtime thefts, and Principal Wilson knew immediately that this was not going to be the average parent-teacher conference. When he saw the haggard and worn look in the woman's eyes, he got it. When she explained that her son wasn't a bad kid but that things had been kind of tough at home lately and that money and time were both in short supply, he listened. When she said that she and her husband were both stuck with new shifts at work and that meant neither one of them could make Billy lunches, let alone drive him to his guitar lessons, Principal Wilson cared. He knew what it was to come home to an empty house, to have to fend for yourself. And even though Billy's allergic reaction to whatever was in that sandwich wasn't dangerous and had been easily remedied with a little Benadryl, Principal Wilson was confident that the experience had gone a long way to scaring the school's lunch thief straight.

Still, Billy had to be disciplined. In this zero-tolerance age, Principal Wilson had a lot of severe options to choose from:

suspension, expulsion, police involvement. All of which would be, sadly, commonplace for a kid prone to bullying.

But Principal Wilson believed in reform over retribution. He preferred to fight fire with water as opposed to more fire. And he knew that suspending Billy, expelling him, or dumping him in detention wouldn't fix anything. The boy would still be angry, and he'd still be taking that anger out on everyone else one way or another. Luckily, Principal Wilson was known for his creativity.

"I think," he said slowly, "I may have a solution."

Meanwhile, Oliver couldn't help but notice how relaxed the lunchroom was today compared to, well, every other day of middle school so far. It was as if the entire sixth grade had taken one big lion-sleeps-tonight sigh of relief.

He also couldn't help noticing how kids kept sneaking looks at him all during lunch.

"What do you expect?" Frankie said. "You dropped the class bully with a peanut-butter-and-jelly sandwich. That kind of thing gets noticed."

Like most sixth graders, the last thing Oliver wanted was to stand out. But throughout the afternoon, he felt like other kids were always watching him, whispering about him.

Then at the end of the day, he closed his locker and turned smack into Matilda.

"We need to talk," she whispered.

"What? How long were you standing there?" Oliver started, but Matilda had already taken him by the arm and yanked him into a nearby empty classroom.

"Matilda," Oliver tried again as she shut the door and killed all the lights in the room. "Where have you been the last few days?"

"Running down leads," she said matter-of-factly as she went to the window.

"You mean, you were skipping?" Oliver asked.

"Chicken noodle soup in the toilet. Basic fake flu," Matilda said, her attention focused more on whatever she saw outside than Oliver's questions. "Yes, Oliver. I was skipping." She turned away from the window and looked at him. "I was doing it for you."

"Matilda, I'm having an even harder time than usual understanding—"

"You're being followed," she cut in.

"What?"

Matilda pulled him over to the window.

"Black Lincoln Town Car, southwest side corner."

Oliver peered out from the side of the window. "Ummm, okay. Yeah, I see it."

Matilda led him away from the window to the teacher's desk,

where she turned on the desk lamp and opened up her composition book.

It was a logbook, a very neat and meticulous daily accounting of anything and everything that Matilda had deemed suspicious or unusual going back months, years even. It was amazing, both in an impressive and kind of unnerving way.

"Well, I've *been* seeing it," Matilda said, pointing to several entries in the log. "Every day for the last two weeks."

"Matilda, it's probably just a parent picking up their kid."

"No dice," Matilda said dismissively. "I ran the plates."

"You *ran* the plates? How did you—"

"Doesn't matter," she said. Then, remembering something, she went back to the window. "Where's the other one?" she muttered, her brow furrowing.

She stood by the window, puzzled, then shook it off and went back to Oliver, taking her smartphone out of her pocket and showing it to him.

"Do you recognize either of these two men?" she said, handing him her phone. The first picture was a surveillance shot of a big, broad-shouldered man with a confused look on his face. The second man was smaller and looked like a ferret who had just eaten some convenience store sushi.

"No," Oliver said. "I've never seen either of these men before."

"Are you sure?" Matilda pressed. "Oliver, it's important."

"Matilda, stop it. What is going on?"

Matilda put the phone back into her pocket. "Okay, like I said, I ran the license plates on the Lincoln Town Car, the one that's out there now."

"Yeah? And?"

"And I got nothing."

"What? What do you mean you got nothing?"

"I mean *nothing*," she said. "At all. Those plates aren't registered. That car doesn't exist, legally that is. So last week I tailed it."

"You what? Are you nuts?"

"I followed it. And that's when I realized that this car has been following *you*. To and from school, every day."

"Me? No way."

"Yes way, Oliver. Along with *another* Lincoln Town Car that has fake plates as well. They're working together, these two men. It's a classic front-and-follow technique, that's how come you didn't notice."

Oliver was so confused he didn't know where to begin. Those men were stalking him? In cars that didn't, legally at least, exist? And what the heck was a front-and-follow technique? Eventually he settled on, "But why are they following me?"

"That's what I've been trying to figure out," she said, flummoxed. "I don't get it, Oliver. Whoever these guys are, they mean business. But near as I can tell, you and your mom are clean."

"What? Clean? Of course we're clean!"

Matilda thought for a moment. "Was your mom ever a whistle-blower against a major corporation or government agency?"

"She does freelance marketing."

"Anyone in your immediate or extended family work for the CIA, NSA, or DOD?"

Oliver sighed. "No."

"Silicon Valley? Mafia ties?"

"No!"

"Well, I'm stumped, Oliver. It just doesn't make any sense."

"It makes even less sense to me, I promise you that."

Matilda checked the window again.

"All right," she said with a sigh. "We'll figure this out, Oliver. Don't you worry. But for now, we better just get you home. We can take the south exit near the faculty parking lot."

She started for the door, but Oliver didn't follow.

"Matilda?" he said. "Don't you think this all sounds a little, I don't know, far-fetched?"

Matilda cocked her head toward the window. "You tell me," she said.

CHAPTER FOUR

Frankie Gets a Job * The Other Car * Trust the Math *
Archie * George Kaplan, Game Changer * More than
an Egghead

Frankie waited around in front of the school as long as he could, meaning as long as he could before he felt awkward and stupid enough that he gave up and started walking home by himself.

He made a detour past Henry's Market, which was now swarmed with middle school kids looking to buy the Billy Fargus–repelling mango-chutney jam, and went inside to get a soda.

Frankie drank the soda too fast. He was still angry and confused that Oliver was a no-show after school. They always walked home together; it was weird.

About a block or so past the market, it got quiet. He'd turned onto a side street, away from the traffic, and was the only person on the sidewalk, on either side of the street. Frankie got a tingly feeling up the back of his neck, one that said he was being watched or followed. He started walking more quickly, but in that way a person walks when they don't want to *look* like they're walking more quickly.

A block or two later, Frankie could hear the sound of quick, light footsteps behind him. They were getting closer.

Then he heard breathing. Low, heavy breathing.

Frankie turned his head warily to find the breathing belonged to a dog. Not just any dog, but a massive rottweiler. The beast was ferocious. It looked like it should be guarding the gates of Hades. Worse, it looked hungry.

Frankie made the mistake of locking eyes, and the dog charged. Frankie shrieked in a key he didn't know he could reach anymore as he took off down the street. He ran as fast as he could, which, he was embarrassed to discover, wasn't very fast at all. His first glance backward revealed that the dog had already closed the gap to a few feet.

Frankie tried to kick into a higher gear, but the dog was already on him, attacking high and knocking Frankie to the ground with an ease that might have been a bit insulting if it weren't so terrifying.

The last refuge of any prey is to curl up in a ball, cover the softest bits, and whimper, and this is precisely what Frankie did.

The dog's massive snout poked and prodded him several times but, curiously, didn't bite. It soon settled on Frankie's backpack, but when it couldn't remove that, it stopped altogether, stepped back, and barked expectantly at Frankie.

After a quick inspection of his personal parts, Frankie noticed that the dog's tail was wagging eagerly as it sat, more or less still, in front of Frankie.

Like it wanted a treat.

"Good boy?" Frankie tried.

The tail swung faster as the massive dog did a little hop with its front feet.

Frankie had a hunch now. He went into his backpack and pulled out the beef jerky Oliver had given him at the market. The dog remained sitting at attention, but its whole body vibrated with carnivorous anticipation as two waterfalls of drool cascaded down either side of its mouth.

Frankie broke off a piece of the jerky and fed it to the dog, who took it, to Frankie's surprise, with gentle care. By the time the dog had gobbled down the last of the jerky, Frankie had a friend for life. He checked the dog's tags and found its name to be *Archie*. There was an address, too. It was a bit of a walk, but in the general neighborhood.

Archie led the way to a very grand, very old house currently in the middle of some massive renovations. Workmen were coming and going when Frankie and Archie arrived. Frankie was just about to ask one of them if the owner was at home when he heard, "Archie! Oh, thank goodness!"

A man in khakis and a dress shirt came running out the front door. Archie met him halfway, at the bottom of the porch. The man crouched down and hugged Archie tightly, his relief apparent. The man then noticed Frankie and stood up, holding out his hand.

"Steve Bishop," the man said. "I cannot thank you enough for finding him."

"Frankie Figge," Frankie said, shaking the man's hand. "Not a problem."

"The workmen keep leaving the back gate open. And Archie likes to explore." Steve dug into his wallet and pulled out a couple of twenties. "Here, please. Let me give you a reward."

Frankie waved away the bills. "That's okay, really."

Archie started nudging Frankie for attention. Frankie crouched down to roughhouse with the massive canine.

Steve watched them for a moment. Then he said, "You know, Frankie, I work in the city, sometimes late. I could really use someone to come and walk Archie in the afternoon. Maybe feed him dinner, hang out with him a bit. Would you be interested?"

Frankie's eyes lit up. "Really?"

"I'd pay you, of course," Steve clarified.

Frankie's face worked overtime to hide any tells that he would have gladly done the job for free. "Um, yeah. Okay. I think we can work something out, Mr. Bishop."

"Steve, please," Steve said. "Now, it is a lot of responsibility. Think you can handle it?"

"Well, Steve, I do know how to close a back gate."

Oliver and Matilda had almost reached Oliver's house when Matilda yanked him behind an oak tree.

"What are you doing?" Oliver asked.

Matilda pointed to a black Lincoln Town Car parked in front of Oliver's house. "That's the other one," she whispered.

They watched in silence for a couple of minutes. When nothing happened, Oliver decided he had to go inside, whether it was the smart move or not.

But then the front door opened, and he saw his mom step outside onto the porch, along with a tall, handsome man in a business suit. Even from a distance, the man was the kind of person you couldn't help noticing. He had an easy, effortlessly confident way about him, like he was used to things going exactly the way he expected them to.

Seeing as pretty much nothing in the past year had gone the

way Oliver had expected it to, a part of him couldn't help but be, at least begrudgingly, impressed.

Oliver instinctively stepped out from behind the tree, but Matilda pulled him back again.

"No. Wait," she pleaded. "That guy looks dangerous."

The man was saying something to Oliver's mom. Oliver feared the worst, but then he saw her smile. And laugh. Were she and the man *flirting*?

Oliver and Matilda watched as Oliver's mom walked him to his car. She handed him a flash drive, which he put in his shirt pocket. Then he patted his pocket as though promising her he'd stored it for safekeeping, and they laughed again. They shook hands, holding on just a half second longer than necessary. *Oh man*, Oliver thought. They *were* flirting.

As soon as Oliver's mom went back inside and the Lincoln Town Car was out of sight, Oliver bolted across the street. Matilda barely caught him before he got to his house.

"Matilda," Oliver said, irritated. "Let me go."

"You can't tell her, Oliver."

"What?" Oliver said, appalled. "She's in danger. You said so yourself."

"She'll be in even *worse* danger if she knows," Matilda said. "Trust me, Oliver."

"That's easy for you to say. It's not your mom."

Matilda let go of him. "We need to figure out what it is that these people want. And our only advantage right now is that they don't know we're onto them."

"What, then? I just have to pretend like everything's fine?"

Matilda paused, considering her next words carefully. "Something tells me you've had a little practice in that department," she said.

Oliver scowled but didn't contest the point.

"There you are!"

Oliver and Matilda practically jumped as they turned around to find Frankie standing behind them.

"I waited forever for you, Oliver," he said, irritated. "Seriously not cool."

Frankie's idea of what was "not cool" expanded considerably after Oliver and Matilda told him what they had been up to for the last hour and change.

"Are you nuts?"

"It's true, Frankie," Oliver said. "I saw it with my own eyes."

"Yeah?" Frankie said, shooting a dubious look in Matilda's direction. "Saw what, exactly?"

"Listen, I know you think Matilda's a little strange and, well, she kind of is." Oliver gave Matilda an apologetic look. "Sorry," he said.

"Not a problem," Matilda said.

"But I believe her," Oliver said. "I really do. Someone's spying on me and my mom."

"Fine. If you really believe her, then why don't you guys just go to the police?"

"Because knowing and proving are two different things," Matilda said. "Until we have more to go on, we can't possibly turn to law enforcement."

Oliver gave his best friend a pleading look. He understood why Frankie wasn't buying it. Heck, he was barely buying it, and he'd seen it all for himself.

"You know what? You guys go do what you want," Frankie said, walking away. "I don't care."

"Frankie," Oliver called after him.

Frankie turned back. "You know what I did this afternoon? I got a job. Dog walking. Ten bucks a day, five days a week. So if it's all the same, I think I'll just go ahead and grow up. But you two feel free to go bust all the spy rings in the neighborhood."

"I know you're being sarcastic," Matilda said. "But there could be legitimate national security implications here."

"Yep, good luck saving the world there," Frankie said as he waved and walked away.

Matilda stomped her foot in frustration. "He is so obstinate."

"It's not too late to change your mind."

Preston looked up from his calculations, checked his watch, and said, "Yes, it is."

Marie frowned. He knew that look—she wasn't going to let it go. "You're putting those children in danger."

"They were in danger already," Preston said. "They just didn't know it."

"But, Preston—"

"I know, Marie," he snapped. "Whatever it is you're about to say, I know."

Preston looked to Tesla, hoping for an ally. But, as always, there was no sign of life from the portrait.

"A year, Marie," he said at last. "A whole year I've been working on this."

"That's precisely my point, Preston. A whole year, just you and your numbers. At some point you're going to have to come out of hiding and trust people again . . ."

"Yes, well, for now I'll stick to trusting the math."

Frankie didn't get mad very often, so he wasn't very good at it. On the one hand, he didn't want to deal with Oliver and Matilda and their wackadoodle conspiracy theories, and he sure wasn't thrilled about the fact that Matilda was now a daily part of his life. She sat with them at lunch and walked with them between classes. She was part of their group, whether Frankie liked it or not.

On the other hand, Frankie wasn't spiteful enough to stop hanging out with his best friend altogether nor vindictive enough to be outright mean to Matilda in the hopes that she would go away and leave them alone.

Instead Frankie settled on a compromise: He spent the school day in a foul and generally antisocial mood. He didn't talk much at lunch, or at all, actually. Sometimes the only verbal interaction he would have with Oliver and Matilda was a "Hey" in the morning and a "See ya" after school when he went his way and they went theirs.

Walking Archie quickly became the best part of Frankie's day. Away from the chaos of his family and the nonsense at school, he could finally relax. It was all but impossible to be angry around Archie. The dog was one hundred and thirty pounds of fur, joy, and unconditional love.

Frankie took him around the whole neighborhood. The dog had boundless energy and could walk all day. For the first few days, Frankie would come home with his legs sore and muscles burning from the miles of exercise they weren't used to getting.

The first day Frankie walked Archie, the dog nearly yanked Frankie's arm off going after a stray cat. They were rounding the corner at the top of a very long, steep hill overlooking the city's warehouse district. An orange tabby darted out from behind some trash cans, across the sidewalk, and toward the street. Archie lunged with such force, Frankie was literally lifted off the ground. He nearly fell flat on his face as he took desperate, lunging strides while a barking Archie leaped in pursuit.

The cat barely escaped by dodging under an old Cadillac parked right at the crest of the hill. It was one of the really old ones, with the big tail fins and everything. Archie tried to go under the car as well, banging his head on a tire block wedged in front of the back driver's-side tire.

Frankie worried the dog might be hurt, but Archie shook off the blow and looked up at him as if to say, "Can we do that again?"

Frankie made a mental note to avoid the street in the future.

After the walks, Frankie would hang out with Archie at Steve's house. He'd feed Archie, brush him, play with him. As much as he enjoyed having a dog, even on a loaner basis, he also lingered at Steve's because he didn't want to go home until he had to. He felt bad about it, but he just didn't want to be around the noise, the mess, the dirty dishes, and baby toys everywhere.

Not that his parents noticed. As long as he made it home by dinner, they didn't care. Even if he did come home earlier, all they'd do is make him watch the twins, clean up around the house, *help out*. And he did that all the time anyway. He just needed a break.

"His name is George. George Kaplan," said Oliver's mom. "And he moved here from Seattle. He started a venture capital firm but recently sold it so he could be closer to family."

"And you met him at the coffee shop?"

"Yeah, right? We just started talking."

Oliver didn't like where this conversation was going, but he laid out plates and silverware on the table anyway. Mrs. Figge had dropped by with another test meal and was putting the food on the plates while Oliver's mom filled her in on the handsome, confident man who apparently drove the *other* Lincoln Town Car.

"Oh, and the best part is that he has a friend in town who runs a software design firm and he may have some work for me!"

"No way!" Mrs. Figge exclaimed.

"I gave him a flash drive with my portfolio on it. He sent it to his friend, and now we're meeting for coffee tomorrow to discuss the project. It's a short-term gig, but it would pay really well."

Oliver remembered Matilda's directive about pretending everything was fine. "That's great news, Mom," Oliver said, trying to force some enthusiasm into his voice.

"A real game changer, huh?" Mrs. Figge said.

"Could be," Oliver's mom said, crossing her fingers for luck. "Heaven knows we could use one."

George Kaplan lowered the headset he'd been holding up to his ear. "Who is the other woman?"

Gilbert checked his notes. "Elaine Figge," he said. "Subject's best friend."

Kaplan nodded. "And the boy . . . Oliver? What's he been up to?"

"Missed him coming out of school today," Gilbert said.

"Really?" Kaplan said, mildly curious.

"You said soft surveillance, so I didn't go looking for him."

"Quite right," Kaplan agreed.

"The lady certainly seems to like you, boss," Sullivan said, putting down his own headset.

George Kaplan smiled with false modesty. "My dear Mr. Sullivan. What's not to like?"

"I suppose you'll be needing me to pose as the software guy?" Gilbert said.

"No, Mr. Sullivan will handle that," Kaplan said. "I need you to go to Detroit."

"Seriously?" Gilbert groaned. "But I just got back from Indianapolis."

"I get to be a software designer?" Sullivan asked eagerly.

"Yes," Kaplan said.

"Really?" The big man bounced in his seat at the prospect.

"Just keep the talking to a minimum." Kaplan sighed. He was already beginning to regret the choice. "In fact, I'll type you up something."

"Fine." Sullivan pouted.

George Kaplan turned his attention back to Gilbert. "Stay the night. Actually, make it two." He handed Gilbert a credit card. "Use this."

"The Feds have this one?"

"They should."

Gilbert put the card in his pocket. "I don't get it, though," he said, working his purple tension ball. "What's so special about Floss Beane anyway?"

"Well, Mr. Gilbert," George Kaplan said. "Before she was

Floss Beane, she was Floss DiCamillo. And Floss DiCamillo is the key to finding Preston Oglethorpe."

"What I don't get," Sullivan chimed in, "is how one egghead could be worth all this trouble. I mean, we've been searching for this Oglethorpe guy for over a year already."

George Kaplan looked at his employee with a mixture of pity and patient condescension. "Egghead?" he said, shaking his head dismissively. "Mr. Sullivan, Einstein was an egghead. Descartes was an egghead. Newton, Aristotle, Galileo, Hawking, all of them fall under the category of egghead. Preston Oglethorpe is something light-years beyond."

Kaplan could see that while his henchmen weren't challenging this assertion, they weren't quite sold on it, either. "Imagine you could destabilize an entire economy with the change you have in your pocket. Or start a war with nothing more than a leaky ballpoint pen."

Gilbert started squeezing his tension ball faster, a sign that he was thinking. "Oglethorpe can do that?"

Kaplan nodded. "Oh yes. He most certainly can."

"I still don't get it." Sullivan, both literally and metaphorically, lacked his own purple tension ball.

Kaplan went with a different approach. "Mr. Sullivan, I imagine at some point you've played Mouse Trap? The game where the little silver ball knocks over one thing, which knocks over another thing, which then knocks over another little silver ball, which knocks over still yet another several things, until finally a big net falls on the mice?"

"Yeah, sure."

"Well, simply put: We're the mice."

Gilbert, catching on, stopped squeezing his tension ball.

Sullivan, not quite there yet, said, "Who?"

"All of us, Mr. Sullivan."

Sullivan's brow furrowed in confusion. "Then who's Preston Oglethorpe?"

"The man who builds the trap."

CHAPTER FIVE

Plenty of Time to Be Scared Later * Shady Glades * A
Dubious Move * Steve Catches On * The Scary Lady in Room
217 * Frankie Stops Keeping Score * Mystery Date

"Okay," Matilda said, jotting down notes in her composition book as they walked to class. "We have 'George Kaplan,' 'Seattle,' and 'venture capital firm.' Anything else?"

"They're going out to dinner on Friday," Oliver said. "To celebrate."

"Celebrate what?"

"He hooked her up with a software company that's farming out some market research."

"So it's a freelance gig? I'm assuming she'll be paid as an independent contractor."

"I don't know," Oliver said, confused.

"Is she going into an office or working at home?"

"Home."

Matilda nodded. "Smart," she said. "They'll probably pay her out of an LLC. Still, it would help if I could get a look at the check. Do you think—"

"No, Matilda!" Oliver cut her off. "Because I don't care about checks and LC whatevers—"

"LLC, it stands for limited—"

"It doesn't matter! Look, I really, *really* don't want her going out to dinner with this guy," Oliver said. "We have to tell her before Friday."

"We've been through this, Oliver. We can't tell her. Not yet. We couldn't even get Frankie to believe us, and he's your best friend. There's no way an adult would listen."

"But she could be in danger."

"It's just a dinner," Matilda said reassuringly. "The danger won't come until sometime later."

As with many of Matilda's attempts to reassure Oliver, this observation produced more panic than confidence.

"By then we'll have a plan," she followed quickly. "I promise. Now, I'm pretty sure everything this George Kaplan told your mom is a lie."

"You say that like it's a good thing."

"It *is* a good thing, Oliver," Matilda said with conviction. "The more he lies, the quicker we can catch him in one and expose him. You need to watch him and listen carefully. Remember every detail. Eventually he'll slip up."

Principal Wilson was making Billy volunteer three afternoons a week to work off his crimes against Preston Oglethorpe Middle School, and he'd given Billy three choices about where he could do it. The first was an animal shelter, the second was a library, and the third was Shady Glades Retirement Community.

Shady Glades was Billy's third choice, by a wide margin. But it was on the way home from his mom's work, so she could pick him up after her afternoon shift at the restaurant. And the cafeteria at Shady Glades would feed him dinner for free. So Shady Glades it was.

Billy went to Shady Glades straight after school on Mondays, Wednesdays, and Thursdays. He started his shift by going room to room and emptying all the wastepaper baskets. That wasn't so bad, as long as he made a point not to look at the trash inside the wastebaskets as he emptied them. Old age should remain a mystery as long as possible.

But with his earbuds in and a good playlist on his phone, the time passed quickly. He could usually get through all the rooms in about an hour, give or take. It depended on whether the resident was around or not. When they were, they sometimes wanted to talk to him. You didn't really have a choice when that happened. The facility director, Mrs. Gonzales, made a point of saying how important it was to be polite and friendly to the residents. That was the only thing she seemed to be really uptight about, so Billy figured it was the one thing he'd better make sure he got right. If he didn't, and she ratted him out to Principal Wilson, he'd end up back in trouble, and he couldn't do that to his mom. Not again.

As a result, Billy got to know most of the residents after the first week or so. Except for the one in room 217. She always kept her door closed, and when he knocked and asked if she needed her trash emptied, she just yelled at him to go away.

Which was fine by him.

Matilda's dad was at the kitchen counter making a sandwich when she got home from school.

"Hey, sweetheart," he said as she came in the side door to the kitchen.

"Hey, Daddy," Matilda said, giving him a quick side hug. "How was your trip?" He'd left two days ago on another work trip—Matilda didn't know where.

There was a lot Matilda didn't know. She didn't like that.

"Oh, long. And boring," her dad said dismissively.

Or perhaps evasively.

When Matilda first spotted the black Lincoln that was tailing Oliver Beane to and from school, it was an accidental discovery. She hadn't even been looking for suspicious vehicles outside her middle school. In fact, she had been sitting under a tree, busily tallying figures in her composition book in the hope of cracking another mystery altogether.

Her dad's new job.

Matilda's father was an FBI agent. They'd moved to the Midwest because he'd accepted a promotion in the Chicago office. This was all fairly routine. For the last few years, Matilda's life had consisted of her father getting promoted and moving around the country pretty regularly.

But something about this move wasn't quite adding up. For starters, the town they were living in. Lake Grove Glen was a nice town, not too big, not too small, lots of trees. But it was a good hour from the city in light traffic, which made for one long commute. Furthermore, Matilda couldn't remember her parents ever talking about where they would live. Moving to Chicago proper was never discussed nor, for that matter, were any of the dozen or so Chicagoland suburbs that would have been more practical options for a small family like theirs. There had been no question that they would move to Lake Grove Glen.

Even a person as naturally suspicious as Matilda could admit that this wasn't much to go on. But there were other things that made Matilda uneasy. Her dad was almost always home for dinner, despite the monster commute. He wasn't getting that many calls from the office, either. When he did get one, he would scowl before he even answered his phone. He took all his calls in his office, closing the door and talking in a low voice.

It sure didn't add up to another desk job. Matilda feared her dad was back in the field. And being back in the field meant he was back in danger.

Matilda was not okay with that.

"You don't have to do this."

"Yes. I really do, Frankie," Steve Bishop said as they walked up the steps to Frankie's house.

Steve had been pressing to meet Frankie's parents ever since he'd hired Frankie to walk and dog-sit Archie, but Frankie had always begged off. Finally, when Steve insisted that, at the very least, he and Frankie's parents swap phone numbers, Frankie knew he had to come clean.

"It's not that big a deal," Frankie protested.

"You have to see it from their point of view," Steve said, more worried-angry than angry-angry. "For the last week, you've been spending your afternoons in a strange man's home—"

"You're not a strange man," Frankie said.

"To them I am!" Steve said.

So now Steve insisted that they both explain the situation to Frankie's mom.

"I still can't believe you didn't tell them," Steve said when they reached the porch.

"I forgot," Frankie said, which even he knew was such a lame excuse that it practically didn't count as a lie. He hadn't forgotten to tell his parents that he'd taken a job walking a neighbor's dog. He hadn't told them because, quite frankly, he didn't want to. It was *his* job. He'd gotten it all on his own. These days, it was pretty much the only thing that felt like it was still just his.

"Besides, it's not like they've noticed," he grumbled.

Steve gave him a look.

"Fine," Frankie said as he opened the front door.

The door to room 217 was open.

Billy Fargus stopped in the middle of the hallway. He was so stunned that he let go of his trash trolley, which rolled a few feet away from him before he caught it.

Then he crept to the door and knocked. There was no answer. He knocked again and slowly, hesitantly, poked his head in the room.

"Hello?" he said. "I'm here to dump your trash for you."

No one was there.

What *was* there, on a stand in the far corner of the room, was a Gibson Les Paul. One-piece mahogany neck, ebony finish, the Black Beauty herself. Billy couldn't help himself; the guitar pulled him inside. It took all his self-control not to touch it, to pick it up.

Billy looked around the room. Two gold records and a vintage playbill for a rock show in London hung on the wall above the bed. On the dresser, several framed pictures of snarling figures in leather jackets and torn clothes stared back at him. The pictures were old, most were black and white, and Billy thought he recognized some of the people in them. Mostly they were men, but one woman with spiked black hair was in all the pictures.

Billy returned his gaze to the playbill on the wall and suddenly it clicked . . .

"Oi, what do you think you're doing in my room!"

Billy knew that he should be afraid. The furious look on the woman's face suggested that when she was done with him, he'd be grateful for whatever punishment Mrs. Gonzales would dream up for him for snooping around one of the rooms. But not only wasn't he afraid, he couldn't stop himself from smiling, now that he knew who the mystery resident of room 217 really was.

"Hey! I'm talking to you, you little—"

"This is you!" Billy said, picking up one of the pictures on the dresser. "You're Bad Becky!"

"Put that down!" the woman growled.

Billy did as he was told.

The woman gave Billy a suspicious look. "You know who I am?" she said.

"Are you kidding? My parents have all your albums. I've got you on my phone, too."

He went to show her his phone, but she made a disgusted face like he should put it away. "Yeah, I know," he shrugged. "Nothing beats vinyl, but what are you going to do?"

She just stared at Billy, not saying anything as the boy swayed a little from right to left. He wasn't used to feeling giddy or carrying the lion's share of a conversation. "Um, my name's Billy. Billy Fargus," he said, extending his hand.

The angry lady looked at it for a moment, then took it. "Becky Tillman," she said.

"It's great to meet you, ma'am. Really," Billy said. "But aren't you kinda young to be in assisted living?"

"It ain't the years, kid. It's the mileage."

"Sorry for intruding," Billy pressed on. "I came to empty your trash and saw your guitar. Is it a '59?"

"Nope. It's a '58," she said warily.

"Wow. Third humbucker and all? Sorry . . . I play. Well, I used to."

"Used to," Bad Becky said. "You don't anymore?"

Billy shrugged. "I had to quit. My dad got moved to nights, and my mom's on days. So now I can't make my lessons."

Bad Becky's scowl softened into something that was, well, still a scowl, but one tinged with empathy for the little trespasser.

He'd dodged a bullet, but Frankie was in a sour mood. For the last half hour, Steve and Frankie's mom had been sitting on the couch, drinking iced tea, and yammering away like old friends. His dad was out running errands with the twins, so at least he'd only had one potentially angry parent to contend with.

Fortunately, Frankie's mom took to Steve immediately and gave her after-the-fact blessing to the dog-walking arrangement. Unfortunately, she *really* took to Steve and jumped at the chance to show him all the latest pictures of the twins.

Frankie was helpless, left to sulk on the love seat while Steve and his mom gabbed away.

"About six months ago, my then fiancée and I decided to make the big suburban move," Steve was saying. "We bought this great fixer-upper over on Maple—"

"Ooh," Frankie's mom cooed. "The Cape Cod?"

"That's the one. Anyway, two weeks after closing, she dumps me for our real estate agent."

"You've got to be kidding! That's terrible!" his mom said enthusiastically.

Steve shrugged. "So now it's just me and Archie. And a steady stream of contractors, plumbers, electricians, and landscapers."

Frankie should have felt relieved. The meeting couldn't have gone better. But there was just one thing Frankie's mom still wanted to know.

"So," she said to Steve as he was leaving, "I'm guessing you're single now?"

Frankie was mortified. This was exactly why he hadn't wanted to mention the job to his parents. There was no need for his worlds to intersect. Couldn't he just have one thing that was his alone?

"Laying it on kinda thick, weren't you?" Frankie said when he and Steve were standing on the sidewalk in front of the house.

"I wasn't," Steve said. "Your mom's nice. And that iced tea was amazing."

"Whatever," Frankie said. "Fresh mint. No big deal. You didn't have to ask to see my baby pictures, too."

"You got off easy," Steve said, walking back to his car. But then he turned back. "I think not telling her hurt her feelings, though," he said. "For what it's worth to you."

Frankie could tell Steve wasn't scolding, just being honest.

When he came back in the house, Frankie's mom was on the phone, so he went up to his room and plopped onto his bed.

His dad returned with the twins a short while later. Pretty soon, Frankie got a knock on his door.

"Your mom tells me you got yourself a job," Mr. Figge said from the doorway.

"She's mad, isn't she?" Frankie said.

"No, not mad," his dad said, stepping into the room. "Interested. And we both think it's great that you took initiative. But you know you can't keep us out of the loop with stuff like that, right?"

"I know," Frankie said. "I was busy. Like you're always busy, between the twins and your new catering business, and I figured . . ."

"You feel taken for granted."

"No," Frankie said reflexively. But then, didn't he? Wasn't

that, maybe, what really bothered him? Everyone assumed that he was game for whatever they wanted from him. Need cardamom? No problem, send Frankie. Forget his plans to play spy with Oliver and Matilda? Sure, why not. Even the twins, with their whole "Frankie, watch!" business, treated him like he had nothing better to do than drop everything when they called. "I mean, yeah. I do, actually."

Frankie's dad sat down on the bed. "I'm sorry, son," he said.

"It's not a big deal," Frankie said.

"No, it is. And I want to hear about it."

"The thing is, sometimes I worry that I might be, well, a pushover. The kind of person no one takes seriously. You know what I mean?"

"I think I do," his dad said. "But I promise you that your mom and I take you very seriously. And we appreciate everything you do for this family."

"Sure, but that's what people always say to a pushover, isn't it?"

His dad chuckled. "I suppose so."

"Then how do you know?"

"How do you know that you're appreciated by the people in your life?"

Frankie wasn't sure until he heard his dad say as much, but that was exactly it. That was the question that had been bothering him lately every time he stepped foot in the house. "Yeah," he said.

His father was silent for a long moment. "I wish I had a simple answer. That there was a mathematical formula to calculate an even exchange between how much we give versus how much we get. But life doesn't work out as neatly as that. Sometimes we give more than we take, and sometimes we take more than we give. But, I find, as long as you have people in your life that you can really count on, it all pretty much works out in the end."

Frankie got the sense that his dad wasn't just talking about him but also about himself. And his mom. Because if he took a step back and looked at things, his parents were always giving more than they were taking. His dad ran himself ragged doing double-duty with his catering company and being a stay-at-home parent. And his mom put in all those long hours at the lab to keep a steady paycheck coming in. And neither one of them was keeping score; they just counted on each other.

"Is Mom okay?" Frankie said.

"Oh, she's fine," his dad said.

"I screwed up. I'm sorry."

"I wouldn't worry about it," his dad said. "Besides, I think you actually gave her a little project. God help us all."

Oliver's stomach had been in knots all week, but by Friday afternoon it was practically doing backflips in his gut. His mom was upstairs with Mrs. Figge, getting ready for her date with a mysterious stranger who had been stalking them for God knows how long. So when the doorbell rang and Oliver got up to answer it, his knees literally buckled.

"Good evening," said the handsome, dashing man in what even Oliver could tell was a very expensive suit. "My name is George Kaplan. You must be Oliver."

The man extended his hand and smiled warmly. Oliver took it.

"Okay. Um, come in," he managed. Then, remembering Matilda's directions to play it cool, added, "Please."

"It's a pleasure to meet you, Oliver," Mr. Kaplan said as he stepped inside the house. "Your mother speaks very highly of you."

Oliver smiled, a little embarrassed. Even though a voice in the back of his head was saying "don't buy it," there was something about this Kaplan guy that made you want him to like you.

"Well, she's my mom," Oliver said. "They're supposed to do that."

"True," Mr. Kaplan said. "But they don't always."

Though the man's tone was light, Oliver got the sense that there was something personal behind the remark.

"Um, my mom's still getting ready," Oliver said, leading Mr. Kaplan into the living room. "Would you like to sit down?"

"Might as well. Gives us a chance to talk," the man said, taking a seat on the couch. "You're in sixth grade?"

"Yes, sir," Oliver said. "Just started a few weeks ago."

"Oh my," Mr. Kaplan said with a chuckle. "Sixth grade. Not the most flattering memories for me, I can tell you that."

"Really?"

"Very awkward time," Mr. Kaplan said. "For everyone, I imagine. Kids who haven't had their growth spurt feel tiny and insecure, while the ones who have feel huge and, well, insecure, too."

"Which were you?" Oliver said.

"Well, probably more the second category," Mr. Kaplan said thoughtfully. "I'd almost reached my adult height by seventh grade, but I had no meat on my bones. I was really just a big head with pipe cleaners for arms and legs. Not a good look."

He laughed, and Oliver did, too.

"More than that, though," Mr. Kaplan said, "it's the time everything seems to change. It's like—"

"It's like you start seeing the world for how it really is, instead of how you thought it was always going to be," Oliver said, finishing the thought.

Mr. Kaplan looked at Oliver, impressed. "Exactly," he said.

Oliver could practically hear Matilda urging him to keep Kaplan talking. "So, um, my mom says you work in venture capitalism. That's, like, investing in small companies you think might become big companies, right?"

"That's right, Oliver. And well put."

"How do you know?" Oliver asked, genuinely interested.

"You mean which ones to bet on? Well, most people will tell you it's all about crunching the numbers. Graphs, charts, statistics, and all that. And sure, that stuff is important. But if you ask me, the only thing you really need to know is how this thing works," George Kaplan said, tapping the side of his temple.

"The brain?" Oliver said.

"The brain," Mr. Kaplan said. "If you know how people think, the numbers will take care of themselves. Every time."

"So how *do* people think?"

"I'm glad you asked, Oliver," Mr. Kaplan said in a cheesy salesman voice. He was having fun with this, and so was Oliver. "Human behavior isn't really that hard to predict. It comes down to four elements: what people want, what people need, what people think they want, and what people think they need. With me so far?"

"Sure," Oliver said.

Mr. Kaplan looked around the room, his eyes settling on a plastic water bottle on the kitchen counter. "Perfect," he said, grabbing the bottle. "Water," he said. "Everyone needs it, right?"

"Right."

"And people have a virtually limitless supply, right there at the kitchen sink. It couldn't be easier to get. In fact, it's so easy to get that people not only don't want it, they don't even drink enough of it. But if you do this," he said, dangling the water bottle playfully in his hand, "it changes everything. When people see the bottle, suddenly they notice a limited amount of water, and they think, *I need that*. And if you put something on the bottle that tells them this water is special, that it comes from a remote mountain spring or a Polynesian island, people will think . . ."

"I want that," Oliver said, getting it.

"Yes!" Mr. Kaplan exclaimed, very pleased. "Congratulations, Oliver. That's all you need to know to take over the world."

Oliver couldn't recall an adult ever speaking to him with such frankness. His own father certainly never had. Mr. Kaplan didn't have to go to such lengths to explain what he did for a living. But he respected Oliver's interest and returned it in kind. And in the process, Oliver had impressed him, and that felt good.

Just then, Oliver's mom came downstairs with Mrs. Figge. She wore a black dress and her hair up, and Oliver was taken aback by how pretty she looked. But it wasn't only the clothes or the hair or the makeup. She looked happy, like for the first time in a long while it was okay for her to feel good about herself.

After Mrs. Figge left, Oliver's mom gave him the rundown about homework, television, and bed, and then she and Mr. Kaplan left for dinner. Oliver watched them walk to his Town Car, where Mr. Kaplan opened the door for her and said something that made her laugh as she stepped inside.

Then as he walked around to his side of the car, he looked back at the house and spied Oliver watching from the bay window. If Oliver were a character in a movie, one of those old thrillers, this was when George Kaplan would lock onto Oliver with a sinister look that implied he was violently insane and there was nothing Oliver could do about it.

But he didn't. Instead, he gave Oliver a little wave that seemed to say, "Wish me luck?"

And, despite himself, Oliver did.

CHAPTER SIX

Frankie's Back ✱ A Brief Appreciation of the Busybody ✱
Mr. Lindo ✱ Archie Misses His Nemesis ✱ Dead End ✱
The Tie That Binds ✱ Google Maps Don't Lie

"I don't know, Matilda," Oliver said as they unpacked their lunches. "Mr. Kaplan seemed pretty nice."

"His story won't hold for long," Matilda said confidently. "They never do."

"But maybe it's not a story," Oliver tried. "Maybe he really is just some guy from Seattle."

"Oliver, don't go all wobbly on me."

"I'm not," Oliver said, a little wobbly. "I'm just saying that my mom . . . she's kinda happy now."

"All the more reason why we can't slack off," Matilda said. "With your mom's guard down, we need to up our game."

"I agree," Frankie said, plopping down in the chair next to them. Oliver practically did a double take.

"You do?" Matilda asked hesitantly.

"Absolutely," Frankie said. "I've been thinking. And the way I see it, if Matilda's right, then you and your mom are in danger. If she's wrong, then we just waste a few days making fools of ourselves." Frankie took a bite of his sandwich and leaned back in his chair, impressed with his own logic.

"Um . . . thanks, Frankie," Matilda said.

"Okay, then," Oliver said. "What's next?"

Matilda gave the question serious thought (well, as serious as a person can be while holding a juice pouch). "Does this Kaplan guy carry his wallet in his pants or his jacket?"

"What? Jacket, I think. Why? Hey, wait a minute," Oliver said, catching on. "No way!"

"If I can get a look at his driver's license, it would really help."

"Are you crazy?"

"Just take a picture of it on your phone and put it back. Easy."

"Right," Oliver said. "Easy."

Matilda, overlooking his tone, turned her attention to Frankie. "Now, Frankie. Your new dog-walking job is the perfect cover for recon and surveillance."

"It is?"

"Definitely. It's a good bet that these people have set up their base of operation within a two-mile radius of Oliver's house."

"So, you want me to walk the dog two miles in every direction looking for black Lincoln Town Cars."

"Very good, Frankie," Matilda said.

"I'm not just another pretty face," Frankie said.

Matilda said, "A concentric pattern around the neighborhood would be most efficient—" She stopped herself, aware, perhaps, of her tendency to be a little bossy. "Actually, for now just try to change your route from day to day, if you can . . ."

She trailed off as she noticed several kids had started holding up their sandwiches in a kind of salute to their table. "Guys," she said, a little unnerved. "Why are people doing that?"

The boys looked around. Oliver's head sagged. "I just wish they'd stop already."

"Seriously?" Frankie laughed. "You haven't heard?"

"Heard what?" Being out of the loop was clearly a new and not enjoyable experience for Matilda.

"I can't believe it," Frankie said, surprised. "You're like the only person in school who doesn't—"

"I've been a bit distracted, lately," she snapped.

"Okay, okay," Frankie said, dropping it. "You know how Billy Fargus lost all feeling in his face a couple of weeks ago after taking Oliver's lunch?"

"Yeah . . ."

Frankie laughed, eager to tell the story to someone new. "Well, it turns out it was the jam on Oliver's sandwich that took him out. Something in it gave him an allergic reaction."

"Jam?" Matilda said skeptically.

"Mango chutney," Oliver said. "It's not like I knew."

"It was awesome. He wasn't seriously hurt or anything, but his mouth went numb for a good hour. And he did get busted for swiping lunches. I hear he has to do volunteer work at the old folks' home three days a week to keep from getting expelled."

"Wow," Matilda said pensively. "Jam. Imagine the odds."

Elaine Figge walked up the front steps with a welcome-to-the-neighborhood basket of pastries in one hand and the elbow of her younger sister in the other.

"I can't believe I let you talk me into this," Josie said.

Elaine, who would be the first to admit she could be a bit of a busybody, looked at her sister and said what every busybody in human history has always said. "It'll be fine. You'll see."

She rang the bell. There was a lot of barking. Then the door opened.

"Elaine, hello," Steve said.

"You're sure this is an okay time?" Elaine said.

"Oh, sure," Steve said. "I'm just waiting on the electrician." He turned his attention to Josie. "Hi, Steve Bishop," he said, offering his hand.

Josie took it. "Josie," she said, smiling awkwardly.

"Oh, silly me," Elaine said, smacking her forehead with her palm. "This is my sister, Josie."

"Would you guys like to come in? I have coffee, we could crack open this basket."

"We would love to," Elaine said, leading her sister inside, but not before turning back and whispering, "See, I told you he was cute."

"Better, but you're coming in late off the bridge," Bad Becky said flatly.

"I know," Billy said, kicking himself. They'd only been at it less than a week, and Billy couldn't believe how much he'd learned. They'd been the best days of his life. Still, he wanted to prove himself, and he took every mistake hard.

"You'll get it," Bad Becky said. "Or you won't."

She always tacked that on, like a gesundheit after a sneeze.

Billy guessed it was because her mouth wasn't used to saying encouraging things, so when she did it felt odd.

"Go again from the top?" Billy said, but Bad Becky's attention was drawn to the door, where Mr. Lindo was standing with a blank, searching look on his face. He was a widower from the memory care wing and the only resident at Shady Glades who got along with Bad Becky, probably because he could never remember that he didn't really like her, either.

He'd been wandering by a lot lately, whenever Bad Becky was giving Billy one of his guitar lessons in the rec room. At first it was kind of creepy, the way the old man just stood in the doorway, motionless. He'd stare at them—and sort of past them at the same time—until one of the attendants came to lead him back to his room.

Once, Bad Becky had even barked at him. "Well, Chester, you in or out?"

He wandered away that time. And the next two times after that.

But today Bad Becky had that look in her eye. The one that meant she was gearing up to yell at the next person she caught in her sights.

"All right," she growled under her breath. Then, with the furious intensity of a Spartan drill instructor in an itchy tunic, she yelled, "Chester Lindo, I've had about enough of your foolishness. You hear me? Get your skinny, wrinkled butt in here. Now!"

Mr. Lindo straightened up and walked directly into the room.

"Drummers. They're all the same." Bad Becky sighed. "You got your sticks?" she barked at Mr. Lindo.

Mr. Lindo nodded quickly, pulling two drumsticks out of his back pocket.

Bad Becky looked around the room. "Billy, slide that round four-top over here."

Billy dragged the table into the center of the room. Becky grabbed a chair as well.

"C'mon, now," she said to Mr. Lindo. "You're holding up rehearsal."

Mr. Lindo sat down at his improvised drum set.

"Ready when you are," Bad Becky said.

What happened next may have technically been just drumsticks banging on a dining table, but it was pretty amazing. Mr. Lindo had been, still was, an excellent drummer. And despite his age and dementia, he kept perfect time.

And for the first time, Billy wasn't late off the bridge.

Archie was pouting again. Frankie couldn't figure it out, but it had been going on for a couple of weeks now. Everything would start out fine. Frankie showed up at Steve's house after school, and Archie would greet him at the door, practically knocking him over in the process. Then they'd head out for their afternoon walk.

But about ten minutes in, Archie's mood would change. His head would hang, and he'd start lagging. It was like he didn't even want to be on the walk anymore. And Archie loved walks.

After a couple of days, Frankie even pinned down the exact point on the walk where Archie started pouting. It always began at the corner before the really steep hill, the one with . . .

. . . the cat.

Could it be that simple?

Frankie doubled back and went down the street he'd been avoiding ever since Archie nearly concussed himself against the old Cadillac parked on top of the hill. Sure enough, the minute they turned down the street, Archie's ears perked up and he went on high alert.

Frankie remembered too late to tighten his grip on the leash. Archie lunged as the tabby they'd seen on their first walk darted across their path and under the Cadillac, hiding like it had before under the tire block behind the rear wheel. Frankie stumbled forward as Archie bounded around the corner of the car, barking enthusiastically. The rottweiler really wanted to get at that cat.

"Come on, boy," Frankie said, pulling Archie back. He

stooped to peek under the car, afraid that the cat, now cornered, might go on the offensive. But the tabby wasn't hissing or hunching. In fact, its orange fur was down; it didn't even look afraid.

Meanwhile, Archie kept barking. But as Frankie listened, he realized that there wasn't any bass, no deep growl behind it. This was a "hey, let's play!" bark.

Frankie had been altering his route per Matilda's instructions. But the next day, Frankie took Archie down the street again first. Archie and the tabby played the same dash, lunge, tire-block, hide-under-the-Cadillac, bark-repeatedly game as before. That's what it was, a game.

And Archie was happy again.

In a way, Archie kind of reminded Frankie of his twin brothers. Whenever he saw the cat, he'd let out a series of four barks and one delighted howl that sounded eerily like Seamus and Hugh's call-and-response battle cry: "Frankie! Frankie, Frankie! Frankie, WATCH!"

It deflated Frankie to realize that he was the cat in the equation. But for the first time since his parents had brought them home, he considered the possibility that his little brothers weren't actually out to destroy him. And though Frankie was still fairly certain that they would someday land him in the emergency room, he was kind of okay with that.

Today Archie's walk took them past Henry's Market. As usual, the place was doing a brisk business. Ever since Billy Fargus had gotten laid out by a peanut-butter-and-jelly sandwich, the little market had been crowded with kids grabbing artisanal jams as soon as they hit the shelves. Curiously, the popularity of the jams didn't drop off after Billy Fargus stopped being the notorious lunchtime marauder of Preston Oglethorpe Middle School. Because while the kids may have initially come for the bully repellant, they came back because it was really, really good jam.

According to a human-interest story in the local paper, the owner, Henry Beecham, had no idea why his homemade artisanal jams were suddenly the hottest ticket in town. And it wasn't just kids flocking to the store, either. Not lately. Foodies from as far as Gary, Indiana, and Kenosha, Wisconsin, had driven in just to buy some of his jam. Apparently, his flavors were even trending on social media.

As Frankie passed by with Archie, he wondered what Henry Beecham might think had he known that his popularity all started because of an allergic reaction to chutney. Probably the same thing Frankie thought when he realized he was walking Archie right now because the same market had been handing out free samples of beef jerky.

Imagine the odds.

"Man, I'm beat," Frankie said on their way home from school. "That dog doesn't quit. Half the time I wind up jogging with him just to keep up. Another couple weeks of this and I'm gonna have legs like a marathon runner. No black Lincolns, though."

"Well, I'm not having much luck, either." Matilda sighed. "I can't figure out why George Kaplan would be interested in Oliver's family. Neither of Oliver's parents seem to be significant."

"Um, ouch," Oliver said. He was getting used to Matilda's dispassionate way of putting things, but a kid does have his pride, after all.

"So, what now?" Frankie asked.

"Well," Matilda began, "now it's up to Oliver."

"Oh no," Oliver said, physically backing away from them. "I can't."

"We're at a dead end, Oliver. Just a peek inside Kaplan's wallet could be a treasure trove of intel."

"Yeah, Oliver," Frankie said. "Matilda here can probably run his picture through some top secret government face-recognition software she's got lying around the house."

Frankie laughed. Matilda didn't. "We're not there yet," she said. Then, to Oliver: "You can do this."

Oliver was not so sure about that.

His mom had been seeing Mr. Kaplan a lot over the last

several days. Oliver knew he was supposed to keep an eye on them, that his mother might be in danger. But at the same time, she seemed really happy, and seeing his mom happy now reminded him of just how unhappy she'd been for this last year. Between Oliver's dad leaving them and everything else with her job and the house, didn't she deserve to feel good about things for a change? Even if it might be a lie?

Mr. Kaplan arrived at five minutes to seven to pick up Oliver's mom for dinner. Oliver let him in with a smile he was sure gave away his plan completely.

"Good evening, Oliver," Mr. Kaplan said warmly as he stepped inside.

"Hi, Mr. Kaplan," Oliver said, fighting a tremor in his voice.

Mr. Kaplan draped his sport coat over a dining room chair.

"Um, my mom will be down in a minute."

"No rush. Actually, could I use your bathroom?"

"Oh, yeah. Past the kitchen, on the right."

Mr. Kaplan excused himself, leaving Oliver alone with the jacket. He'd never get a better chance.

Oliver took his cell phone out of his pocket and opened the camera app. That, of course, was the easy part. Then, after a quick look down the hall, he pulled back the coat lapel to see Mr. Kaplan's wallet resting comfortably in the inner right breast pocket.

Oliver held his breath as he sticky-fingered the wallet and removed the driver's license and credit cards. He then managed to photograph the license and two of the cards before he started to get light-headed. He had been holding his breath. Oliver exhaled and took another deep gulp of air, as if he were performing this amateur spy act underwater.

Once the wallet was safely back in the sport coat, Oliver looked up, sure that Mr. Kaplan would now be standing before him with a none-too-pleased look on his face. But he was still alone in the living room; he'd gotten away with it.

Which is what made Oliver's next move all the more foolhardy. It was a nice jacket, a very nice jacket; Oliver had noticed it when he let Mr. Kaplan in the house. Oliver wasn't much for clothes, but Mr. Kaplan had looked so at ease wearing it. So put together.

In control.

He had to try it on and get just the briefest idea of what it was like to feel those things.

It felt good.

"The coat works on you," Mr. Kaplan said.

Oliver turned to see Mr. Kaplan watching him from the hallway.

"I—I'm sorry," Oliver stuttered. "I was just . . ."

"You need the full effect, however," he said as he closed on Oliver in two long, easy strides. When he reached Oliver, Mr. Kaplan removed his tie.

"Turn to the window," Mr. Kaplan said as he stood behind Oliver, lifting the collar on Oliver's shirt and draping the tie across Oliver's neck. "Thin on the left, thick on the right," Mr. Kaplan said patiently as he began tying the tie, checking their work in the window's reflection.

"Of course, this tie doesn't really go with your shirt," he said as he fixed the dimple under the knot. "Though these days, mixing patterns is trendy. So, what do you think?"

Oliver and Mr. Kaplan looked in the window. Oliver forgot everything about the black Lincolns and the likelihood that this man, who let him wear his expensive coat and had just taught him how to tie a tie, was probably not who he claimed to be. He wanted to enjoy the moment, for this to be real.

"I think it's perfect," Oliver's mom said from the bottom of the steps.

"Oh, Floss." Mr. Kaplan turned. "Oliver and I were just goofing around." He gave Oliver a conspiratorial wink. "I'll tell you what, Oliver. Keep the tie for practice. I'll need the coat back, though." He leaned down and stage-whispered in Oliver's ear, "It's got my wallet."

Had Mr. Kaplan offered up a kidney or some spare bone marrow, Oliver couldn't have felt any lower. He took off the coat and handed it to Mr. Kaplan.

"Frankie! Door stays open!" Frankie's mom called from downstairs.

"It's open, Mom," Frankie called back from his bedroom.

Oliver and Frankie had arranged for Oliver to come for a sleepover while Oliver's mom was on her date. Matilda came over as well and was currently synching up Oliver's pictures onto her laptop.

"What are we supposed to do about that?" Matilda said, gesturing to the open bedroom door.

"Don't worry," Frankie said, dismissively. "The twins pretty much scream and spill things for two hours straight after dinner. My folks will have their hands full until at least eight o'clock."

As if on cue, one of the twins shrieked as the sounds of loud objects falling shook the entire first floor of the house.

"Okay," Matilda said, typing furiously on her laptop. "Let's see what we got."

Oliver and Frankie watched in amazement as various web

pages popped up on the screen, many of which seemed like the type that weren't exactly open to the public.

"Wait a minute," Frankie said, squinting at the screen. "Did you just hack into the Seattle DMV website?"

"Yes," Matilda said plainly, as if she'd been asked if George Washington was our first president. She frowned, disappointed. "Hmmm. The license is legit."

"So Mr. Kaplan's telling the truth?" Oliver said, perking up.

"Not necessarily." Matilda resumed her furious typing. A Google Maps snapshot of a Starbucks in downtown Seattle popped up on the screen. "Yep. Here we go."

Oliver and Frankie leaned closer.

"What's that?" Frankie asked.

"That," Matilda said with a smug air of satisfaction, "is the home address listed on Mr. George Kaplan's driver's license."

"A Starbucks?" Frankie said. "Oh, I get it. Fake address, right?"

"I knew he'd slip up. Sooner or later they always get lazy with the little details." Matilda stopped as she noticed that Oliver had receded away from them. He sat down on Frankie's bed, a dejected look on his face.

"This is good, though. Right?" Frankie said. "I mean, now we know."

"Yeah," Oliver said, conceding the logic. "You're right. Now we know."

But he couldn't let the sinking feeling go. It followed him through a half-hearted game of Clue, a couple of hours in front of the TV, and a chocolate-chip-cookie break down in the kitchen. Pretty soon, it was time for Matilda to go.

"When I get home, I'll start running through Kaplan's credit card statements," Matilda said as she and the boys waited on the porch for Matilda's mom to come pick her up. "If we know where he's buying his gas and his groceries, we should be able to narrow our search grid considerably."

"Yeah, cool," Frankie said, trying to sound upbeat. Oliver had hardly spoken since they'd learned the truth about George Kaplan.

Oliver knew his friends were worried about him, but he also doubted that he could explain to them how or what he was feeling. Because the truth was, he almost felt more sad than afraid. He had really liked Mr. Kaplan, even when he was suspicious of him. And Oliver really thought Mr. Kaplan liked him, too.

He knew it was foolish. Deep down Oliver had never doubted that Matilda was right about Mr. Kaplan. So why did he let himself fall for the man's act? Even for a second? Maybe because, for a brief moment or two, everything seemed okay again. Mr. Kaplan made Oliver's mom happy for the first time in a year, and he made Oliver feel like he wasn't disposable, that he was worth the time it takes to teach a boy to tie a tie. Because even if Mr. Kaplan was some kind of mysterious archvillain, he at least knew that Oliver and his mom were too important to throw away for a personal trainer in Phoenix, Arizona. Oliver believed that, and maybe believing it made it easier to overlook the lies.

Matilda's mom pulled up in front of Frankie's house. Matilda grabbed her backpack and computer. "See you guys on Monday," she said.

Halfway down the steps she stopped, turned, and ran back up the steps to Oliver and gave him a hug.

"Oh," Oliver said, taken aback.

"They say a ten-second hug can completely reboot a person's emotional biorhythms," Matilda said, holding on to him firmly. Then, about four seconds later, she said, "There," and let go of him.

He did feel better, though a little awkward. Matilda must have felt awkward herself, because she gave Oliver a sudden but not unkind punch in the arm. Then she ran back down the steps.

CHAPTER SEVEN

Looking for Mr. Kaplan * Please Don't Stop the Music *
Photographs and Memories * Oliver Has a Hunch * Imagine
the Odds * A Not So Simple Google Search * Matilda Goes
Dark * Butterflies, Chaos Theory, and the Third Kid

Matilda spent the weekend going through all of George Kaplan's purchases, and by Monday she had a search grid of roughly ten square blocks.

"It's a lot of ground, I know," Matilda said as she pointed out the shaded area on the grid map laid out on the cafeteria table. "But I'll bet anything George Kaplan lives somewhere in there."

Frankie leaned over the map. "Hey, I know that area," he said. "This helps a lot, Matilda."

"Could I come with you when you walk Archie after school today?" Matilda asked. "Get a ground view of the area?"

"Yeah, sure," Frankie said.

"I can come, too," Oliver offered.

Matilda considered. "You better not, Oliver. Kaplan doesn't know us. But if he saw you wandering around his neighborhood, it might tip him off."

"She's got a point," Frankie said.

"Wow." Oliver chuckled. "Well, if you two are finally agreeing on something, I'm not going to get in the way."

That afternoon, Matilda joined Frankie on his walk with Archie. The big dog took to her instantly, licking her face with such overwhelming intensity that Frankie actually heard her giggle.

"What?" she said as she wiped some of Archie's slobber off her forehead. "Did I miss a spot?"

"Huh? Oh, nah, I think you got it all."

About four blocks into the walk, Matilda said, "Are we heading away from the search grid?"

"Yeah," Frankie said. "Have to make a quick detour first."

They approached the old Cadillac on the top of the steep hill. It didn't take long for the orange tabby cat to dart across the sidewalk and under the car. Archie lunged desperately, banging his head into the tire block and snapping his jaws in what even he had to know was a pointless attempt at snagging his prey.

"Oh my goodness," Matilda said, startled. "He nearly caught that cat."

"No, he didn't," Frankie said. "They do the same thing every day. We get about ten feet from this house, then the cat darts from behind a bush right in front of Archie and ducks under this car. That cat's got it timed perfectly."

"Then why do you keep walking this way?"

"I think they both kinda enjoy it," Frankie said. "I figure, give them a little fun. What's the harm, you know?"

They walked Archie for over an hour but only covered a small fraction of Matilda's search grid and spotted no black Town Cars.

"We could spend weeks searching like this," Matilda said, plopping down onto a patio chair in Steve's backyard. "And then, we could walk right past their safe house and not even know it because no one's home."

Frankie filled Archie's bowl with water and sat down as well. "Maybe we're going about looking in the wrong way," Frankie said.

"How do you mean?"

"Well, today we walked all around one section of your search grid," Frankie said. "And spent a lot of time on small side streets that were too far off the main intersections. But what if we could make it so that I stayed on the bigger streets, the ones with more traffic? Then I'd have a better chance of spotting one of their cars as they enter or leave the neighborhood, right?"

"Right," Matilda said. "That's good, Frankie. I could set up a mapping algorithm to give us different search routes to optimize both traffic flow and street visibility."

"Sure," Frankie said with an amiable shrug.

"Sorry," Matilda said. "I mean I could run a program—"

"It's cool," Frankie said. "I got most of it."

Billy Fargus fidgeted in his chair. So did Bad Becky. Billy was so nervous he had to keep reminding himself he wasn't in trouble.

Of course, it would be a whole lot easier to remind himself if Mrs. Gonzales wasn't looking at him like that.

"A band," she said, her tone somewhere between a question and a statement.

"Yes, ma'am," Billy Fargus said.

"With you two and Mr. Lindo?"

"Uh-huh," Billy said.

"You are aware that Mr. Lindo has advanced dementia?"

"Yeah, but it gets better when he plays," Billy said. This was, in fact, true.

"Plays?" Mrs. Gonzales asked. "Drums?"

"Well, now he just taps his sticks on the table," Billy said. "We'd have to get his set out of storage."

Billy realized that this last sentence might be where he officially pushed his luck.

Mrs. Gonzales had been really cool so far. She let him off work half an hour early so that he could practice guitar with Bad Becky in the rec room. And she gave them the room on his off days as well. Billy was now at Shady Glades almost every day after school.

"I might come to regret this, but all right," Mrs. Gonzales said. "On one condition: You have to invite Mr. Abernale to join the band as well."

"What?" Bad Becky practically jumped out of her seat, which, considering her knees, was no small gesture. "No! No! No"—she steamed, scrunching up her face as if it took all the muscles in her skull to keep from swearing—"way!"

"What's the big deal?" Billy said. "Mr. Abernale's a pretty nice guy."

"And a very accomplished pianist," Mrs. Gonzales added reasonably.

"He's a *jazz* musician!" Bad Becky exclaimed.

Mrs. Gonzales was unmoved by the passion of Bad Becky's argument.

"Besides, he won't do it anyway," Bad Becky said. "He hates me."

"So what? Most of the residents hate you," Billy said matter-of-factly.

Bad Becky gave him a look, but she was self-aware enough to know that when you've got a tell-it-like-it-is personality, you have to be able to hear it like it is, too.

"And you don't have to like somebody to make great music with them," Billy plowed forward. "You and Mongo Jenkins hated each other, but you wrote all the best songs on *Brain Batter Bingo* together," he said. "Just saying."

"Uh-huh," Bad Becky said. "Remind me to tell you about the time I broke ole Mongo's nose with a mic stand."

"Those are my terms. Take it or leave it," Mrs. Gonzales said not unkindly.

Bad Becky glared for a moment. She looked over at Billy. Then she glared at Mrs. Gonzales again, just for good measure. "Fine," Bad Becky said, storming for the door in a huff.

"So," Mrs. Gonzales said as Billy followed Bad Becky to the door. "What are you calling yourselves?"

Billy smiled. The name had been his idea. "The Dangerous Jams."

While Frankie and Matilda were on their scouting mission, Oliver went home and tried to act normal. He'd been more or less avoiding his mom since last Friday, when he'd learned the truth (or at least a fraction of truth) about George Kaplan. But Oliver knew she was starting to notice and hoped she would chalk it up to middle school moodiness. A couple of times she'd even asked him if anything was wrong. Kids hate it when parents do that. And parents hate it when kids answer "nothing."

Especially when they know their kids are lying about it. Oliver's "nothing" really was something. Something he desperately wanted to tell his mom. Something he felt rotten not telling her.

Something that was currently in their living room, sitting next to her on the couch.

"Oh yes," Mr. Kaplan said, laughing. "I do love that hair."

Oliver's mom swatted him playfully on the arm. "Hey! Bangs were very in that year."

Oliver had seen Mr. Kaplan's car in the driveway—the driveway, not on the street anymore—and had come in through the kitchen door.

They were looking through an old yearbook and laughing. It was the kind of moment that should have been sweet, but knowing it really wasn't was almost too much for Oliver to bear. The urge to rush into the living room and expose Mr. Kaplan as a liar and fraud was so strong, Oliver felt like his heart was going to beat right out of his chest.

But then what? Oliver knew he couldn't physically make the man leave, and once exposed, Mr. Kaplan might turn dangerous. Oliver had never felt so helpless in his entire life.

"And who's that boy next to you?" Mr. Kaplan said, leaning over to get a closer look at the book in Floss's lap. "Preston— Oh my word. Is that Preston Oglethorpe? The physicist?"

Floss nodded. "Yes, it is. He used to live down the block from me."

"Amazing," Mr. Kaplan said, regarding the picture again. "You two sure look awfully chummy."

Oliver watched as his mom turned away just a little, both from the book and the man. "We were, actually," she said. She was quiet for a minute. "But then, well, you know. I went to eighth grade and he went to—MIT, I think it was."

Mr. Kaplan started to say something else, but then Oliver's mom finally spotted him in the kitchen.

"Oh, Oliver," she said, dumping the yearbook onto Mr. Kaplan's lap and straightening her skirt as she stood up to greet her son. "I didn't see you there."

"Hey, Mom," Oliver said, forcing a lighthearted smile onto a face that clearly didn't want it there.

"Oliver, hello," Mr. Kaplan said, rising and offering his hand. After much internal debate, Oliver took it.

"I'm surprised you aren't over at Frankie's," said his mom.

"I know," Oliver said. "I have a lot of homework tonight, so I just came home."

"Very responsible," Mr. Kaplan chimed in.

"Okay," his mom said. "Want a snack or anything?"

"No, thank you," Oliver said. "I'm just going up to my room. If that's okay?"

"Sure, honey," his mom said.

Oliver tried not to run up the stairs, but it wasn't easy.

An hour later there was a light knock on Oliver's door.

"Got a minute?"

Oliver looked up from the homework he wasn't really doing. "Um, sure, Mom."

She came into the room and sat on Oliver's bed. He turned in his chair to face her.

"This afternoon, with Mr. Kaplan," she began. "It bothered you, didn't it?"

"Mom . . ."

"It's okay, I get it," his mom said. "I mean, I know this must be weird for you. Me . . . dating, I guess you could call it. I know it's weird for me."

Oliver nodded but didn't say anything. He was supposed to

say that he wanted her to be happy. He *wanted* to say that he wanted her to be happy because, well, he really did want her to be happy. More than anything. But if he said that to her now, she'd think he was saying that he wanted her to keep seeing Mr. Kaplan.

"Okay," his mom said, a patient, understanding smile on her face as she stood up. "I'm going to start dinner."

She left him there, alone in his room, feeling rotten. She would probably break it off with Mr. Kaplan if he asked her to. But again, that might back the man into a corner, and he might react badly.

If only they could figure out what he was after.

I know this must be weird for you.

"Weird." The word hung there in his mind. Something *was* weird this afternoon. It wasn't just seeing Mr. Kaplan and his mom cuddling next to each other on the couch—though that was definitely weird. It was something else.

Something about Mr. Kaplan was different today. Oliver felt like he'd spotted a crack, however small, in the man's smooth, effortless veneer.

They had been looking at old pictures, an old yearbook of his mom's. That was kinda odd. Oliver didn't even know his mom had kept her old school yearbooks. They had a stack of photo albums in the bottom row of the bookcase, but his mom wasn't really one of those stroll-down-memory-lane types. Especially not since Grandpa died. Or since she and his dad got divorced.

Had it been Mr. Kaplan's idea to dig up her old yearbooks? The more Oliver thought about it, the more he remembered how Mr. Kaplan had seemed way more interested in them than his mom was. In fact, she kind of seemed to be humoring him.

Why would this guy want to look through some old yearbooks?

After dinner, Oliver went into the living room. The yearbook was still on the coffee table, opened to the last page his mom and George Kaplan had been looking at. There was the picture of his mom. She was around Oliver's age, maybe a little older, her arms around two boys on either side of her. And all three of the kids had big smiles on their faces.

Oliver read the caption:

Best pals Jimmy, Floss, and Preston

Preston Oglethorpe. The famous scientist, the guy they named Oliver's school after.

Mr. Kaplan had made the connection pretty quickly.

Maybe because he'd already known about it.

"Okay. So I'm standing in line at the dessert buffet and trying not to eavesdrop on these two women," Frankie's aunt Josie was saying. Frankie was cleaning up from dinner while his aunt and his mom had coffee at the kitchen table.

Aunt Josie had come over straight from some work mixer for Steve's firm. It was the fourth date Aunt Josie had had with Steve, if you counted the welcome basket she and Frankie's mom had brought to Steve's house a few weeks back. Aunt Josie clearly did.

Ordinarily, Frankie would have tuned this kind of conversation right out. But it was about Steve. Also, whenever someone tells a story about eavesdropping, it's impossible not to start eavesdropping yourself. Like yawning.

"The first woman is all worked up. I mean, really agitated. So she says, 'Two weeks out! Can you believe it? He cancels two weeks out!'"

Frankie's mom refilled their cups and offered her sister the creamer.

"And then the second woman—oh, thanks—the second woman, she says, 'Unbelievable. Angela, whatsoever are you going to do?'"

"Did she really say 'whatsoever'?" Frankie's mom asked doubtfully.

"Nah, but it's more fun that way. Anyway, so the frantic woman—"

"Angela."

"Right, Angela. Angela says, and this is the important part,

'I'll never find a decent caterer in the city to step in this late. Not for one hundred people.'"

Aunt Josie paused for dramatic effect. It worked. Frankie stopped in the middle of drying a sippy cup to give the story his full attention.

"And?" Frankie's mom said impatiently.

"Well, of course I introduced myself and said I just happened to know the best caterer in the greater Chicagoland area."

"You didn't?" Frankie's mom gasped.

"You know I did!" Aunt Josie squealed. "Now, when your husband gets home, you tell him to expect a call from a frantic woman named Angela sometime tomorrow."

"Oh, Josie. This is wonderful. Thank you so much!"

"Are you kidding? I'm thrilled I could help. Talk about a coincidence though, right?" Aunt Josie laughed. "I mean, I just happen to be standing in line behind someone who desperately needs a caterer at the last minute? Seriously, imagine the odds."

Before Frankie's mom could answer, the two sisters were startled by the sound of a plastic sippy cup bouncing off the kitchen tile.

"Whoops, sorry," Frankie said, picking the sippy cup off the ground while trying to shake off a downright dizzying case of déjà vu. "Guess I just got caught up in your story there."

It started with a simple Google search on Preston Oglethorpe. Two hours later, Oliver's head was swimming. The more he read about Preston Oglethorpe, the more Oliver found himself bombarded with complex terms and theories. *Chain reaction simulations. Probability mapping. Causality scenarios. Butterfly effect.*

He'd hit a dozen brainy scientific websites to help him understand it all, then another dozen less-brainy scientific websites to help him understand what the first websites were trying to explain to him.

He sort of followed what they were talking about. But then again, not really.

At ten o'clock, he texted Matilda to see if she was still awake. Four and half seconds later, her face appeared on his computer screen. She didn't FaceTime him or Skype him; she was just there.

How did she do stuff like that?

"Oliver, what is it?" Matilda asked bluntly. "Are you in danger? If you're compromised and can't talk, just type 'daffodil' on your keyboard and I'll—"

"I'm fine, Matilda," Oliver cut in. "Really."

"Oh, okay," Matilda said, sounding almost disappointed. "Um, what's up?"

"I have some links I want to send to you—"

"Got 'em," Matilda said over the furious clicking of her keyboard.

But I haven't even sent them to you yet, Oliver thought. When this was all over, they really needed to have a talk about personal boundaries.

"Wow, this is pretty heavy stuff, Oliver."

"Yeah, I was hoping maybe you could look it over and, well, explain it to me?"

"Sure. But why?"

"I don't know. Just a hunch—"

"Right. Best not to say any more. To avoid any confirmation bias down the road."

"Sure."

"So, Frankie and I struck out reconnoitering this afternoon."

"Huh?" Oliver said, then put it together. "Oh, right. The walk. Well, it would have been surprising if you found anything the first time out."

"Unlikely, for sure," Matilda agreed. "But it wasn't a total loss. I think Frankie's starting to mind me a lot less."

"Mind you?"

"Well, I do tend to get on his nerves."

"Oh, I wouldn't say—"

"Oliver," she said with a directness that ended further debate. "I know I can be a pushy know-it-all sometimes. It's cool. I mean, you can't be a better you until you're truly honest with yourself about who you are. Am I right?"

Man, she's an odd one, Oliver thought. But she was also kind of amazing at the same time.

"Well, even if you are a pushy know-it-all," Oliver said, "you're *our* pushy know-it-all."

"Oh, Oliver." Matilda blushed. "That's very sweet of you to say. Now go to bed. You look tired, and lack of sleep can hinder development in adolescent males."

Oliver looked at the yearbook on his desk. He doubted his mom would come looking for it but decided it might be best to hide it under his bed. However, when he picked it up off the desk, something fell out of the back.

It was a stick, like the kind used to hold a Popsicle or an ice-cream bar. Printed along the side it said:

FAROUK'S FAMOUS FUDGSICLES

Oliver opened the yearbook and found where the stick had been taped to the inside of the back cover. The tape was old and yellow and had no adhesiveness left. He returned his attention to the stick, turning it over to see if there was anything written on the other side.

There was. On the back, someone, most likely his mom, had carefully written:

my perfect day

Matilda missed school for the next day, texting both the boys with a message that read simply: *Shadow protocols. Radio silence. 36 hours.*

"What the heck does that mean?" Frankie said.

"I think it means, 'Don't bother me, I should have something in a day and a half.'"

Frankie reread the text. "Huh, okay," he said.

Sure enough, a day and a half later, in gym class, Matilda plopped down next to Oliver on the bleachers. It was dodgeball day, and Oliver was an early out as usual.

"That was some hunch you had," she said. "Can't wait to hear a little more about it."

Oliver started to speak, but Matilda stopped him. "Not here," she said, looking around furtively. "After school. Frankie's house."

"Paranoid much?" Oliver joked.

"Yes," Matilda said without a trace of humor.

Down on the gym floor, Oliver saw Frankie duck just before a dodgeball took his head off.

"Hey! No headhunting!" Frankie cried. "Coach?!"

Oliver turned back to Matilda, but she was already gone.

Matilda shut Frankie's bedroom door behind them.

"My mom says we have to keep that open on account of you're a girl," Frankie protested.

"I know, and we will," Matilda said, dropping a thick stack of papers onto Frankie's desk. "In a minute." She looked at Oliver. "So, about that hunch of yours? Why Preston Oglethorpe?"

"Preston Oglethorpe?" Frankie said, confused. "You mean the guy they renamed the school after?"

"Yep," Oliver said.

"The one they showed us the video about?" Frankie said. "The genius scientist who disappeared and now no one knows where he's at?"

"Yes!" Matilda barked in frustration. "And are you purposely trying to end all your sentences in prepositions?"

Frankie thought for a moment. "Maybe," he said.

"All right," Oliver said, taking his mom's yearbook out of his backpack. He opened it to the page with his mom and the two boys. "That's Preston Oglethorpe," he said. "And that's my mom."

Matilda took the yearbook and looked closely at the picture. For a long time, she just stared at it quietly.

"Well," she said finally, "the good news is that your instincts were correct. I think I know what George Kaplan is up to."

"Now who's ending their sentences in prepositions?" Frankie quipped.

Matilda took a cleansing breath.

"What's the bad news?" Oliver asked, getting them back on track.

"Pretty much everything else," Matilda said. "At the time of Preston Oglethorpe's disappearance, he was working for a top secret government think tank."

"Okay," Frankie said, his voice cracking a little. "Um, you just used 'government,' 'top secret,' and 'disappearance' all in the same sentence. That cannot be good."

"You didn't happen to get any information on this think tank, did you?" Oliver said.

"No such luck." Matilda scowled. "But Preston Oglethorpe's research was about controlling probability scenarios. He was developing mathematical formulas that could manipulate—" She stopped when she saw how hard the boys were trying to look like they were following her. "Okay," she said, slowing it down. "Either of you two familiar with chaos theory?"

"I loved their last album," Frankie wisecracked.

"This is where it all started to get away from me," Oliver confessed.

"Okay. According to a scientific principle called chaos theory," Matilda explained, "a tiny, seemingly insignificant event in one place can start a chain reaction that causes cataclysmic changes someplace else."

"The butterfly effect," Oliver ventured.

"Exactly," said Matilda.

"Is that like if you go back to prehistoric times and step on a butterfly, it could change the entire course of the earth's history?" Frankie said.

"That's one example," Matilda said. "Another is that the tiny flap of a butterfly's wings on one side of the world could start a series of events that causes a hurricane on the other side."

"Okay . . ."

"Now, imagine if you could create a mathematical equation that told you where to place that butterfly to make the hurricane happen, wherever and whenever you wanted."

"So this Oglethorpe guy was studying chaos theory to control the weather?"

"Not just the weather," Matilda said. "Anything."

"Whoa, hold on," Frankie interjected after double-checking the hallway and closing the door again. "Sorry, but I'm still back on a butterfly causing a hurricane. How does that happen?"

"Well, I guess if it flapped its wings at the right time in the right way, it could push a weather pattern just enough to change it."

"How?"

"I don't know how, Frankie. I'm a cyber pirate, not a meteorologist."

"Is it at least a really big butterfly?"

Matilda stared at Frankie like she was trying to work out whether he was messing with her or not.

"Okay, let's try this," she said after some thought. "Frankie, say one day your mom is taking the twins out in the stroller so they'll fall asleep for an afternoon nap."

"Okay. With you so far."

"And as they stroll past a flower bed, a butterfly flaps its wings, stirring up a tiny whiff of pollen that finds its way into one of your brother's nostrils, causing him to sneeze, which then wakes up your other brother, who starts crying. Now both of them are up and they won't go back to sleep. So your mom brings them home and leaves them with you because she has errands to run and your dad's busy in the kitchen. Still with me?"

"It's like a page out of my life. Keep going."

"Okay, now you have to spend the afternoon watching the twins. But you had planned on using that time to study for your math test, because you have a low C in that class and you really need to pull up your grade."

"For the record, I actually have a mid-to-high C in math."

"Since you don't get to study, you wind up bombing the test, lowering your grade to a D, the grade at which all parents freak out. Your mom and dad hire a tutor, but they make you split the cost to teach you a lesson about responsibility for letting things get so bad in the first place."

"Wow, are you just making this up as we go?"

"Hush. You get a job mowing lawns to help pay for the tutor. Then one day you're mowing a lawn in your old sneakers, the ones with no tread, and you slip while pushing the mower up a small hill. The mower rolls back down and cuts off half your foot."

"Whoa. Dark."

"Obviously, spring Little League is now out. Your parents feel terrible about your injury and bring home a cello for you to play while you recuperate."

"Why a cello?" Oliver chimed in.

"Yeah, why a cello?"

"Really? You guys are hung up on the cello?"

Oliver and Frankie shrugged.

"Okay, then. One of your dad's friends bought it for his daughter, but she never plays it, so he sold it to your dad real cheap. Good enough?"

"Sure," Frankie said, satisfied.

"Wonderful. Where were we? Oh, right. You learn the cello, unlocking a hidden gift for music, and you get good, really good. You practice hours and hours every day, at first to fight off the boredom and to distract yourself from your disfigured foot, but over time you discover a deep love of music. You go to Juilliard and then become a rich and famous classical musician. All because . . ."

"A butterfly flapped its wings," Oliver said in a soft voice.

"That's right."

There were a few moments of quiet while the boys processed all of this.

"And this Oglethorpe dude," Frankie said finally, "he was using math and science and stuff to figure out where to put the butterfly?"

"Metaphorically speaking, yes."

"Is it just me, or is this really scary?"

"It's not you. A person who could manipulate chaos theory like that would be invincible. They could do just about anything they wanted. And the most frightening part of all: You wouldn't even know they did it."

"I'm beginning to see why Oglethorpe disappeared."

"And here's the really scary part," Matilda said, taking a photograph from her stack of papers and putting it flat on the desk for the boys to see. "My guess is that all this time he's been hiding from George Kaplan."

The boys looked at the photograph. It was a grainy, black-and-white shot of a group of scientists standing in a room packed wall-to-wall with supercomputers.

"The young guy front and center is Preston Oglethorpe, all grown up," Matilda said, pointing him out in the picture. He looked to be in his mid-twenties when it was taken, and at least ten to twenty years younger than the rest of the scientists.

"Now look at the guy on the far left."

The boys did. "Holy smokes!" Frankie exclaimed. "It's him! It's George Kaplan!"

Oliver felt his blood turn to ice.

"I don't suppose this photo had a caption anywhere telling us who Kaplan really is?" Frankie tried.

"Unfortunately, no."

Oliver looked at Matilda. "You think Mr. Kaplan is in town because he thinks Oglethorpe is here, too?"

"Yes," Matilda said quietly. "I do."

Frankie caught on as well. "And he's getting chummy with Oliver's mom because she was childhood friends with Oglethorpe. He's—" Frankie stopped, not wanting to finish the thought.

"He's using my mom as bait," Oliver said, his voice little more than a trembling whisper. "Isn't he?"

"Oliver, we're going to—"

"What?" Oliver said, panicked. "What are we going to do, Matilda? Tell me. Because I have no idea. What are we going to do?"

No one said anything for a while. Then Frankie slammed his palm on the desk.

"I'll tell you what we're gonna do," Frankie said. "We're going to get ahead of this thing. We're going to find Oglethorpe first, before that creep Kaplan can."

"Frankie," Oliver said skeptically.

"He's right," Matilda said firmly. "It's the smart play. We can do this, Oliver. I know we can."

Oliver looked at his friends, trying to feed off their optimism. "Sure," he said. "Three kids trying to track down the smartest man in the world. Should be a piece of cake."

Frankie returned to the yearbook. "Hey, guys," he said. "Any idea who this other boy is in the picture? The one with the busy shirt. Jimmy—"

Matilda snatched the book away from him. "He's probably a dead end," she said a bit abruptly. "But I'll keep this and look into it. Just to be safe."

CHAPTER EIGHT

When Shady Glades Is Rocking, Don't Bother Knocking *
Matilda Sandoval Acts Her Age * Imagine the Odds (Part 2) *
The Reluctant Babysitter * Bad Becky Says Please * Frankie
Survives His Brothers * The Telltale T-Shirt

Like any retirement community, Shady Glades had seen its share
of heated battles. Cribbage versus gin rummy, *Diagnosis Murder*
versus *Murder, She Wrote*, tapioca pudding versus Jell-O—these
were the kind of hot-button issues that turn geriatric brother
against geriatric brother.

But one thing that nearly everyone at Shady Glades agreed
upon was that the rec room was the place to be every Wednesday
at five. That was because Shady Glades now had its very own
house band, the Dangerous Jams.

Though Bad Becky would never admit it, Mrs. Gonzales was
right to make them invite Mr. Abernale to join the band. Not

only was he an excellent piano player, but he was the only one who could stand up to Bad Becky when needed. And it was needed a lot. Bad Becky was an amazing teacher—Billy was learning so much and improving so quickly—but she wasn't always the easiest person to get along with.

Mr. Lindo became a new man once they dug his old drum set out of storage. Billy would watch how, over the course of a rehearsal, Mr. Lindo would grow increasingly more alert, more aware. He still got confused easily, but he knew Billy's name now, and whenever they talked music, the old man was always sharp as a tack.

Billy was familiar with the expression "win-win," but he'd never believed such situations actually existed. Yet here it was. Billy was happy. Mr. Lindo and Mr. Abernale were happy. Even Bad Becky was relatively happy. Which meant she wasn't making the Shady Glades staff constantly unhappy, so they all had to be happy, too.

And all because Billy had gotten caught swiping lunches.

Imagine the odds?

"Matilda, where in the world is this coming from?" her mother asked. Her tone fell somewhere between incredulous and very perturbed.

The truth of it was, Matilda didn't know herself. Not an hour earlier she had been picking songs for them to listen to on Spotify while her mom was cooking dinner. Everything was fine. Better than fine, even. Then her dad called to say he'd have to miss dinner, to go ahead and eat without him.

No big deal.

Her mom hung up the phone and said, like she'd done dozens of times before over the years, "Just us tonight, sport. Your dad's stuck at the office again."

Matilda suddenly felt a burning behind her eyes, like when her dad surprised them with pizza. Except now she felt angry instead of sad. They were patronizing her. Mocking her. Treating her like a child.

She'd show them just how childish she could be.

"Really? Is he?" Matilda said.

"Pardon?"

"At the office?" Matilda said, making sure to dump an extra helping of sarcasm onto the question.

"That's what I said." Her mother drew the words out, trying to gauge just what was happening.

"I know you and Dad are keeping secrets from me," Matilda blurted out defiantly. "Don't bother denying it," she added, feeding off the adrenaline rush one gets from an impulsively bad decision.

"All right," her mother said in a "let's do this, then" tone of voice. "Yes, your father and I do keep things from you. You know why? Because we're parents. You're a child, Matilda. You're our child, and I'm sorry to say that there will always be things that we don't tell you. Things that, frankly, aren't any of your business."

"That's not fair," Matilda said, deflating a bit the way all kids do when they realize that they've just fallen back on the three most useless words in any argument. "I am part of this family, aren't I?" she said, regrouping.

"Yes, Matilda. You are," her mother said. "The most special part of this family. But not an equal one." Then, to soften the blow, her mom added: "Not yet."

"So we just all keep pretending everything's okay?"

"You want to go down *that* road?" her mom said. "Fine, let's talk about pretending. Let's talk about that *Moonglow* poster you have up in your room. You've never seen any of those movies. You think they're insipid. So why put the poster on your wall? Who are you trying to fool? Me? Yourself?" Matilda's mother looked at her, searching her eyes. "Maybe it's your way of pretending that everything's okay, too."

Matilda looked away.

"But maybe they're not okay," her mom said. "Maybe things are hard. Which is why last month you poured chicken noodle soup into the toilet so you could skip school?"

For a brief moment, Matilda considered opening up to her mom about how hard moving all the time was. Always being the new girl. Never really fitting in. Because she was really smart and didn't hide it. Because she was a little odd and couldn't hide it. But Matilda knew she couldn't say these things. Because if she did, she wouldn't stop, and then she'd tell her mom everything. About Oliver and the black Lincoln Town Cars and the mystery man courting Oliver's mom. If that all turned out to be nothing, her parents would think she was a total freak.

And if it wasn't nothing, then her dad might get hurt. Again.

Matilda didn't say anything. She went back to making the smart choice. She asked if she could take her dinner into the family room, ate it in front of the TV, then went upstairs to her room and fell asleep in her clothes.

"Hey, guess what?" Frankie said, dropping his lunch on the table and plopping down next to Oliver. "My dad just got this big catering gig in the city."

"No way," Oliver said.

"That's great," Matilda said.

"Yeah, it's a funny story, actually," Frankie said, unwrapping his sandwich. "Turns out my mom set Steve up with my aunt Josie."

"Wow," Oliver said. "Your mom works fast."

"I know, right? Anyway, Steve takes her to this swank party in the city where Aunt Josie starts talking to this rich lady whose caterer had just canceled on her. She mentions Dad and—bam!"

"That's incredible."

"So incredible!" Matilda said. "I mean, imagine the odds."

Frankie stopped eating his sandwich mid-bite. "Wait a minute," he said. "What did you just say?"

"Uh, 'Imagine the odds'?"

"Why?"

"Well, because, what *are* the odds of something like that happening? I mean, it's quite a coincidence. Right?"

"Yeah, right," Frankie said uncertainly. He had a feeling there was something, some connection he should be making. But it was just out of his reach.

"Frankie, what?" Matilda said.

"I don't know. It's probably nothing. Just that my aunt said the exact same thing when she told the story. Which makes sense, 'cause, like, what are the odds, right? But then, I remembered thinking the same thing a few days ago when I was walking Archie past Henry's Market. I thought, 'Imagine the odds.'"

"Why?" Matilda said.

"Because that's where Oliver bought the mango-curry jam that took out Billy Fargus."

"Mango chutney," Oliver corrected.

"Sorry, mango chutney."

"Never mind that," Matilda said shortly.

"Anyway, we'd never been to that market before, and we weren't even there to get jam."

"Why were you there?"

"Well, we were there to get . . ." Oliver started, confused. He turned to Frankie. "Why did we go there?"

"My dad needed cardamom, remember."

"Oh, yeah," Oliver said.

"Cardamom?"

"It's a spice," Frankie said.

"I know what cardamom is," Matilda snapped.

"Right," Oliver said. "Because all the other grocery stores were out."

"Hold on," Matilda said. "All the other grocery stores in the area were out of cardamom? *All* of them?"

The boys shrugged, not yet following her train of thought.

Matilda closed her eyes and laid her hands flat on the table. For several moments, she just sat there thinking.

"Matilda," Oliver began, but she gave him a shush finger.

"I am so stupid," she said, eyes still closed and finger still in the air. Then she opened her eyes and pointed at Frankie.

"How'd you get your dog-walking job?"

"Archie got loose one day because some workman left the back gate open. I found him and brought him back to Steve's house. Then Steve offered me a job walking Archie after school."

"Where did you find him?" Matilda asked.

"He found me, actually," Frankie said. "He started chasing after me. I thought he was going to tear me apart, but it turns out he just wanted the beef jerky in my backpack."

"Since when do you eat beef jerky?" Matilda asked.

"Well, I don't really," Frankie said. "But I got it for free when—"

"—when I bought the jam that took out Billy Fargus," Oliver said hesitantly, getting where Matilda was going with this.

"Okay," Matilda said slowly, piecing it all together. "The beef jerky in your backpack and Oliver's mango-curry—"

"Chutney," the boys corrected in unison.

"—came from the same market. And this is the same day that Frankie's dad ran out of cardamom?"

Oliver and Matilda shared a look. Then it hit Frankie, too.

"Whoa, wait a minute. You guys are saying that Preston Oglethorpe made all that stuff happen."

"Uh-huh," Oliver said.

"So my dad running out of cardamom was like the butterfly flapping its wings?"

"Yep," Matilda said.

"Okay," Frankie said. "Gonna be honest, I'm kind of freaking out over here."

"Wow," Oliver said. "Matilda, I can't believe you figured all that out. That was amazing."

"Thanks, but Frankie here was the one that pieced it together first."

"Me?"

"Of course," Matilda said. "The way you caught me saying 'Imagine the odds'—that was because you were subconsciously making the connection."

Frankie liked the idea that at least somewhere in his brain he was smart. "Thanks, Matilda."

"Just one question, though," Oliver said. "If Preston Oglethorpe is really doing all of this, then . . . why? What's he trying to accomplish?"

Matilda frowned. "I don't know. But when we find him, I'll be sure to ask."

"Josie can't do it, obviously," Frankie's mom said. "And I don't want to risk breaking in a new sitter for something this important."

Frankie's parents were trying to figure out a way for his mom to help out at his dad's first big catering gig. Aunt Josie usually babysat for them, but she'd be running the waitstaff, and his dad could really use his mom there as another pair of eyes to make sure everything went smoothly.

It had been a few days since Frankie, Oliver, and Matilda had decided that they were going to find the smartest man in the world before George Kaplan could. Their progress so far had been, well, minimal.

The last lingering hints of summer were giving way; there was a brisk snap of fall in the breeze. It would be getting dark earlier soon. The slow but steady change of season had been getting to Frankie and his friends lately. Reminding them that there was a time limit to their search, and that time was running out.

However, listening to his parents trying to work out their childcare issues reminded Frankie that he had other people counting on him as well.

"I can do it," Frankie said, the words popping out of his mouth before he'd fully formed them in the first place.

"Pardon?" his mom said.

Frankie took a breath. Volunteering was harder the second time, now that he realized exactly what he was saying. "I can do it. I can watch the twins. That way you can go and help Dad."

"Are you sure?" his mom asked.

"Yeah, it'll be fine."

"Frankie, that would be a really big help," his dad said.

"No problem," Frankie said, trying to keep the growing fear that it would be a complete disaster from showing in his eyes. "I've got this."

As soon as the words left Frankie's mouth, they all heard a bloodcurdling scream from upstairs, followed immediately by a similar but slightly different bloodcurdling scream.

"And nap time is over," Frankie's dad said.

"You're back," Mrs. Gonzales said as she sat down at her desk.

"Yes, ma'am." Billy fidgeted in his seat. As did Bad Becky. "We—um, we got a gig."

"A gig," Mrs. Gonzales said cryptically.

"Yes, ma'am," Billy Fargus said. He went on to explain that the Dangerous Jams had been offered a chance to play at JoJo's Bar and Grill, for money.

JoJo's was an eatery only in the loosest sense of the word—they did have a grill, and occasionally they would burn meat on that grill, slap it between some bread, and call it a hamburger. But it was really just a dirty, rundown hole in the wall that catered to aging roughnecks with a fondness for motorcycles and drinking beer out of the pitcher.

Basically, old people with attitudes.

"JoJo's, huh?" Mrs. Gonzales said. "And are they paying you in tetanus shots?"

Bad Becky barked out a laugh.

Mrs. Gonzales watched Billy sink in his chair. The truth was that she had spoken with Billy's mom about JoJo's the night before and had already offered to chaperone the little outing, per Mrs. Fargus's approval.

But Mrs. Gonzales couldn't let on right away. She had to play the stick in the mud, at least for a little while. After all, she was dealing with someone who had a history of hostility toward others, and she couldn't afford to look like a pushover.

Still, it didn't seem fair to make poor Billy squirm, too.

"What about Mr. Lindo?" Mrs. Gonzales asked.

"Chester'll be fine," Bad Becky said.

Billy took over. "Um, what she means is, we talked with his grandson, and he said it's okay as long as . . ."

"Yes?"

"As long as someone from Shady Glades is there to keep an eye on him," Billy said, trying to make it not sound like a big deal.

"That's a big deal, Billy," Mrs. Gonzales said.

"I know," Billy said.

"It's stupid," Bad Becky piped in. "Chester's not gonna wander off or anything. Besides, he's pretty much all there when he's playing."

"That's true, Mrs. Gonzales," Billy said.

It was. Mrs. Gonzales had seen it for herself.

"And it would mean a lot to him," Billy said. "I know it would, ma'am."

"I understand that. But it would be a considerable expense. We couldn't go short a staff member here, so we'd have to bring someone in on their day off. Pay them overtime, probably . . ."

"You could come," Bad Becky said quietly.

"Pardon?"

"You could come to JoJo's. Ma'am," Bad Becky said. "You're on salary, so it wouldn't, you know, cost anything."

"Except your time," Billy interjected. "Which, we know, is worth a lot."

"Ms. Tillman, are you inviting me to your gig?"

"Yes," Bad Becky said. "Please."

And there it was. Mrs. Gonzales would go down in Shady

Glades history for getting Bad Becky Tillman to say please. This had gone better than she had even hoped.

"Then I would love to come," Mrs. Gonzales said.

Frankie figured his plan would either be a stroke of genius or a gigantic mistake right up there with chili dogs before a roller coaster. When his parents left for the catering job around three, Frankie told his little brothers that if they were good, he had a surprise for them.

To his absolute shock, they were good—they didn't injure themselves or each other, break anything, or try to knock down any load-bearing walls. They even put more of their dinner into their mouths than they dropped on the floor.

Steve showed up promptly at five thirty to drop off Archie. If anyone could absorb the limitless, destructive energy of Frankie's twin brothers, it was a one-hundred-and-thirty-pound rottweiler.

Frankie took Seamus, Hugh, and the dog out back, and for the next two and a half hours, his little brothers hung on Archie, climbed on Archie, chased Archie, threw their bodies at Archie, and even tried to ride Archie like a horse. Though never aggressive with the boys, Archie gave as good as he got, and by eight o'clock the big dog and the savage twins were all passed out on the living room carpet, positively exhausted.

Frankie carried the twins up to their room, one at a time, and tucked them in their beds. On his way out the door, he heard Seamus stir slightly.

"Frankie?" Seamus said, waking just a bit.

"Yeah?"

"Thank you," Seamus said.

"Sure thing. Good night, Seamus."

"G'night, Frankie."

"Frankie, Frankie," a sleeping Hugh instinctively mumbled into his pillow.

Frankie's mom came home just after eleven. The event was a huge success, and everyone loved his dad's food. She thanked Frankie again for helping out.

"It's no big deal," Frankie said, though in truth he was pretty proud of himself for keeping his brothers out of the emergency room and the house in one piece.

"Now tell me the truth," his mom said as she sat on the floor and rubbed Archie's belly. "Was this really just a clever way of showing us how much we could use a dog?"

Frankie laughed. "Nah, I don't need a dog of my own anymore. Archie here might get jealous."

Matilda took out the old yearbook from under her bed again and opened it to the picture of Preston Oglethorpe, Oliver's mom, and the third kid. A boy.

She still hadn't said anything to Frankie and Oliver. She told herself it was because she wanted to be sure first.

But she was sure.

So sure that she didn't even need to check the official class picture to get the full first and last name. She already knew that the third boy in the picture was Jimmy Sandoval.

The third boy was her dad.

She knew because the third kid in the picture, the boy on the other side of a young Floss DiCamillo, was wearing a *Big Trouble in Little China* T-shirt.

So her dad had been best friends with Oliver's mom. And Preston Oglethorpe. It explained a lot. But like most answers, it came with a bunch of new questions.

And Matilda was going to get the answers.

CHAPTER NINE

Black Lincolns and Stop Signs * Kaplan's Real Address *
Finding Oglethorpe * Tesla Speaks * Front and Follow * Oliver
Is Running Out of Time * Five Questions (and One Lie) *
Matilda Crosses a Line

Archie's walk started out like usual. Frankie took him by the
Cadillac at the top of the hill, where Archie made his daily lunge
for the darting cat. Over the last few days, the two had expanded
their little dance. The tabby seemed more playful and had
begun slipping in and out from under the car in a game of
hide-and-seek. Archie, who loved courting injury almost as
much as the twins did, couldn't resist throwing his body into
that rear tire block repeatedly to try to catch his friend. But the
cat was too quick, and Archie always eventually gave up.

Today Frankie took Archie into the last section of Matilda's
search grid. If after today he didn't find the Lincolns or anything

that hinted at where George Kaplan was hiding out, he didn't know what they were going to do.

Frankie walked the blocks and his fears were confirmed when, once again, he came up empty. Dejected, he turned around and started back. He was about to cross the street when, out of the corner of his eye, he saw a car that clearly had no intention of stopping at the stop sign, and he pulled back just in time.

"Hey! It's called a stop—" Frankie started to yell, but then he noticed something.

The car was a black Lincoln Town Car.

Frankie watched as it drove up the block and pulled into a driveway. He walked past the house and subtly checked the license plate. He had a pretty good feeling he knew who it belonged to.

Matilda answered the door to find Oliver and Frankie on the front porch, goofy smiles on their faces.

"I saw one of the black Lincolns," Frankie said. "I found George Kaplan's hideout!"

Matilda hugged them both. "That's great, that's just great!" Then she looked back into the house and closed the door behind her as she joined the boys on the porch.

"It's over on Euclid," Oliver said, handing her a piece of paper. "Here's the address."

"I'll see what I can find," Matilda said, taking the paper. "But I'm sure the registration will be bogus, and we probably won't learn anything new. But, hey. We found George Kaplan! One down, one to go."

"Yeah," Frankie said. "Only I doubt a grid search is going to help us find Preston Oglethorpe."

"Maybe," Oliver said, an idea forming. "Maybe we don't need one."

"Huh?" Frankie said.

"Yeah, I'm with Frankie on this one."

"Think about it. No matter how smart this guy is, if he wants to control the future, Oglethorpe still has to do his research. He had to know that Frankie's dad was a chef and that Billy Fargus was allergic to something in that mango-chutney jam and that the guys working on Steve's house kept leaving the gate open. And he also had to connect those variables to us somehow, right?"

"Right," Matilda said.

"So if Oglethorpe knew that I was about to lose my lunch to the school heavy and that Frankie wanted a dog and that Frankie's dad needed clients for his new catering business . . ."

"Then he had to be close by, watching us," Frankie said. "Closer than George Kaplan."

"Exactly," Oliver said. "Mr. Kaplan just had to keep an eye on me and Mom. But for Oglethorpe to collect his intel . . ."

"He'd need to study us," Matilda finished the thought.

"Study us," Oliver repeated Matilda's words, rolling them over in his mind. He slapped his hand on the porch railing. "That's it!"

Matilda and Frankie looked at him, not following yet.

"School!" Oliver exclaimed. "He's gotta be working at the school."

Matilda thought about it. "That makes the most sense," she said. "Okay, wait here. I'll grab my laptop and then we can go to Frankie's and follow this up."

"Why can't we just stay here?" Frankie said.

Matilda looked back into the house. Her dad was in his office, working. Ever since she saw that picture in the yearbook, the one with Oliver's mom, her dad, and Preston Oglethorpe as kids, she'd been trying to figure out how it all added up—those three kids in the past, and her and Oliver and Frankie in the present—but she was having a hard time connecting the dots. She did have one theory, though. But she didn't like it and didn't want to say anything until she was absolutely sure.

"We just can't," she said, shutting the door and leaving them there waiting on the porch.

Matilda ran upstairs to grab her laptop from her room. She was almost out the door again when she heard her dad say, "Matilda? Are there two boys on our porch?"

Matilda turned around to see him peeking out the window in his den.

"Oh, them," Matilda said with forced nonchalance. "Yeah, we're working on a group project together. For school. Bye, Dad!"

Matilda bolted out the door before he could respond. "Come on," she said, ushering the boys down the steps and onto the sidewalk.

When they got to Frankie's house, his dad made them try some sliders he was working on before they went upstairs. They were really good. So good they almost forget they had work to do.

Almost.

"Okay," Matilda said, sitting down at Frankie's desk, her fingers already dancing across her keyboard. "I'm in the school district database. Accessing Preston Oglethorpe Middle School."

"Oglethorpe disappeared a year ago, so we can rule out anyone who's been at the school longer than that," said Oliver.

"We can also rule out any women faculty or staff," Frankie added.

"Got it," Matilda said, typing away.

"Ooh, don't forget height," Frankie added. "You can't fake short."

Matilda finished typing. "Good, okay. That narrows it down to five men." She pulled up an old photo of Preston, then scrolled through the profile pages of possible Oglethorpes. "Nope. Nope. Definitely not." Then one picture caught her eye. "Hold on."

Matilda clicked on an employee profile of a shaggy man, his face almost completely obscured by thick hair and a scraggily beard.

"The janitor?" Oliver asked.

"Sure," Frankie said, studying the picture. "Could be anyone under there."

"It says he's only been working at the school a few months."

"What happened to the old janitor?"

"Good question," Matilda said, typing away again.

Frankie's mom called from downstairs, asking the kids if they wanted dessert.

"Go ahead," Matilda said. "This might take a while."

Twenty minutes later, the boys returned with a dessert plate for Matilda.

"Any luck?" Oliver asked, handing her the plate and a fork.

"Take a look," Matilda said with the half of her mouth that wasn't full of apple torte.

Oliver and Frankie looked at the laptop screen. It was an article from the local paper with a picture of a hardscrabble but very happy old guy in a casino holding a giant novelty check over his head.

Frankie read the article aloud: "'Local school janitor Eldin Scruggs wins 2.3 million dollars after placing several long-shot bets at the Mirage Sports Casino in Las Vegas.'"

"No way," Oliver said, reading over Frankie's shoulder. "This says he quit his job at the end of the school year and moved to the Bahamas."

"Imagine the odds?" Matilda said with a smirk.

"We've found him," Oliver said. "We've found Preston Oglethorpe."

Not so very far away, Preston Oglethorpe sat at his table, picking distractedly at his dinner.

Beep!

He paid his watch little mind.

"They're close. A week?"

Preston looked up. The Nicola Tesla portrait had come awake.

"Less," Preston said. Then, "I thought you weren't talking to me."

"Don't flatter yourself," the portrait responded. "I just wasn't talking."

"That's a bit of an understatement. You've haven't said a word in months."

"There was no need," he said dismissively. "You already weren't listening to Marie. No sense in piling on. I get it, though. I know a bit about what it means to have an enemy."

"Exactly!" Preston said. "And you beat your enemy. You won the War of the Currents."

"Did I?"

"Of course you did. Your science was vastly superior to Edison's. The whole world uses alternating current. You know they've got electric cars named after you now?"

"I died alone, Preston," Tesla said bluntly. "Half-mad and entirely broke. I isolated myself. I pushed the world away from me. I allowed my enemy to define me. Whatever happens, don't let that man define you."

Preston looked down, the words weighing on him. "Are you telling me to call this all off?"

"I'm telling you that when this is all over, it's time to come out of hiding," Nicola said. "The life of the mind, no matter how brilliant, is no substitute for *living*. When it's time, let the world back in, Preston."

Preston started to respond, but Nicola had already clicked off, and the portrait screen was dark once again.

"This is it?" Oliver asked.

"According to the school records," Matilda answered.

They stood in front of Henry's Market.

"This is where we got the jam and the beef jerky," Oliver said to Matilda.

It was also the home address listed on the shaggy janitor's school employment file.

Business at the market had not let up—if anything, Henry's jams had gotten even more popular in the last few weeks. There was practically a line out the door.

"Is this a joke?" Frankie said.

"I think it's a message," Matilda said. "I'm just not sure if the message is 'you're getting close' or 'you'll never find me.'"

"What do we do now?" Oliver asked. "If Preston Oglethorpe doesn't live here, how do we find him?"

"We go old school. Low tech. Find him at school and tail him home." Matilda's eyes narrowed. "It's time I teach you guys to front and follow."

"Front and follow?" Oliver repeated dubiously.

"It's a pretty simple technique," Matilda said. "When you're following someone, the best approach is to have someone in front of the person and someone else behind. That way the person you're following doesn't get ahead of you, and you can trade off with your partner every so often so you don't get spotted."

"There's three of us," Frankie observed.

"And we'll need it," Matilda said. "Our subject has a car and we'll be on foot."

They started the next day after school. Matilda watched the janitor's car, a beat-up Oldsmobile Cutlass, and followed it out of the school parking lot around five o'clock. When it came to the first turn, Oliver and Frankie were already half a block down the street in either direction.

The first day, they got lucky and the Cutlass caught all the red lights, making it easier for Matilda and the boys to keep up with it. They made it about a mile before the car got away from them.

The next day, Matilda stayed at the school and texted the guys when the Cutlass was on the move. This time Oliver and

Frankie started at the intersection where they lost the Cutlass the day before, making it about a half mile this time before losing the car. It was painstaking and exhausting, but it would have been worse had Frankie not been in such great shape from walking and running with Archie. Though he hadn't quite achieved the legs of a marathoner, his speed and stamina had come a long way in the last several weeks.

By the third day, they had tracked the Cutlass to the warehouse district, losing it in the middle of a dense patch of old, possibly abandoned brick buildings.

"It's gotta be one of these four here," Oliver said later, pointing to the grid map Matilda had spread out across Frankie's bed.

"I agree," said Matilda. "Our janitor's been keeping a pretty consistent schedule, so I figured tomorrow I'd come with you guys. We can wait him out here, in between these buildings," she said, pointing to a spot on the map. "It's got the best sight lines."

The boys nodded. They were all silent for a moment.

"So, tomorrow we meet Preston Oglethorpe," Frankie said.

"Yeah," Oliver said, but there was no excitement in his voice. "Tomorrow, then."

Matilda's expression was grim as well.

Frankie looked at his friends, confused. "Hold on," he said. "I thought this was good. This was what we wanted, right?"

"It is," Matilda said measuredly. "But we can't assume that Oglethorpe is going to help us."

"Why not?" Frankie said. "Hasn't he kind of being doing that all along? Helping us get what we want?"

"Yes, he has," Matilda conceded. "But that's only been for a couple of months. He's been hiding from George Kaplan for over a year. If he has to pick one over the other . . ."

"He might not pick us," Frankie said, completing the thought. "So, are you saying we shouldn't go tomorrow?"

"No," Oliver cut in. "She's just saying don't get your hopes up. We don't know why he's been doing any of this."

"And if this guy is as bad as George Kaplan?"

"It's our only play, Frankie," Matilda said.

"Either way, at least we can make him pick."

Oliver came home from Frankie's to find George Kaplan setting the dining room table.

"Oliver, you're just in time!" Mr. Kaplan said as Oliver walked in the room. "You can help us celebrate."

"Celebrate what?" Oliver managed.

"I got another marketing job," Oliver's mom said, coming in

from the kitchen with a pan of lasagna. "Mr. Sullivan, George's friend, has more work for me."

"He was very impressed with this last project," Mr. Kaplan added. "Your mom really knocked it out of the park."

"I was kind of surprised," Oliver's mom said. "Mr. Sullivan, he's not very forthcoming. Doesn't say much at all, actually."

"He's more of an introspective personality," Mr. Kaplan explained.

Oliver had seen crime movies about cops who had to go undercover and pretend to be bad guys. It was always brutal for the undercover cops, living two different lives, pretending to be different people all the time. Oliver really felt for them. Just pretending that he didn't know someone else was pretending was making his stomach do backflips.

"Wow," Oliver said. "That is great. Congratulations, Mom."

"Thanks, honey," his mom said, hugging him.

"This is just the beginning, Oliver," Mr. Kaplan said, giving Oliver a little wink. "I see great things on the horizon for you and your mom."

Matilda knocked on the door to her dad's office. He was closing some files on his desk when she came in to say good night.

"Sleep tight," he said, kissing the top of her head.

Matilda spied her father's travel suitcase up against the wall. "Another trip," she said.

"Yeah, last minute." He sat back in his chair knowingly. It was time for Matilda's five questions.

"How long?"

"A day or two. Quick."

"Flying or driving?"

"Driving."

"In state?"

"No."

Matilda nodded. She had two questions left. She looked over and saw the *Big Trouble in Little China* movie poster hanging on the wall. "Dad, you moved around a lot when you were a kid, huh?"

"Yeah, a few times," her dad answered. He wasn't sure if they were still doing the five questions. "When Grandpa Joe was doing contract work for the Navy, we bounced around the country a bit."

"Have you ever lived in the same place twice?" Matilda asked. "Like, have you ever gone back to live in one of the places you lived before?"

Her dad thought about it. "No," he said, looking off to the side the tiniest bit. "Not yet anyway."

"Okay," she said. "Okay."

Matilda had thought her dad lying would make what she had to do easier. It didn't. She'd done a lot of things with her computer that were, frankly, illegal, but she'd never felt bad about any of them before. This was something different.

When Matilda went to bed that night, she didn't go to sleep. Instead, she waited until she heard her parents go into their bedroom. Then she waited some more.

And some more after that.

At two o'clock in the morning, she snuck out of her room and down the stairs.

Her dad's office was unlocked, and his laptop lay on the desk, just like always. It was password protected, of course, as was his sign-in to the FBI's criminal database, but Matilda had memorized all her parents' various passwords when she was seven.

She was now, electronically at least, impersonating a federal law enforcement officer. If she got caught, she suspected the fact that the officer in question was her father wouldn't matter.

Matilda uploaded the picture of George Kaplan's bogus driver's license into the database's facial recognition program. Once the upload was complete, she received an estimated response time of twelve to fifteen hours.

By tomorrow afternoon she'd know who Kaplan really was. If all went well, she'd know where to find Preston Oglethorpe, too. And then she'd tell her dad everything.

After tomorrow there'd be no more secrets.

CHAPTER TEN

"Found it," Frankie called from around the corner.

Oliver and Matilda followed him down an alley across from an old brick building that was a little smaller than the other industrial complexes that dominated the warehouse district. It wasn't abandoned necessarily—it had all its doors and windows and looked maintained—but certainly overlooked.

A breeze blew down the alley. A blend of summer and fall air, warmth and coolness rode the same current, as if the breeze could go either way but hadn't decided yet.

"Are you sure this is the right place?" Oliver asked, a lump forming in his throat.

"I saw the Cutlass pull into the rear loading dock," Frankie said.

Matilda, meanwhile, was already casing the building. "There's a door over here. It's unlocked."

Oliver looked at his friends warily. Now that they had trailed their janitor here, he sensed that none of them really knew what to do next. Still, they had come this far and didn't have time to waste. It was already past five and soon their parents would be wondering after them.

Oliver nodded to Matilda, and she opened the door slowly, quietly. She and the boys stepped inside, staying close to the doorway.

Oliver didn't know where to look first. There were computers and screens and scientific equipment, machines that hummed and whirred in strange melodies of computation, old school blackboards filled with the kinds of mathematical equations that look like a foreign, alien language.

"It's like the Bat Cave for nerds," Frankie said.

Beep!

The sound came from the far end of the warehouse. Then, from the same direction, the flush of a toilet, and before they could decide whether to make a run for it or not, a man stepped out from a small, makeshift bathroom.

"Um, hello," the man said. "You're right on time. Well done. My name is, um, Preston Oglethorpe."

He was a gangly, skittish man in faded tweed pants and a clashing, wrinkled dress shirt that had what appeared to be soup stains on the collar. Oliver knew it was wrong, but he couldn't help comparing this man to George Kaplan, the sinister impostor who was deceiving his mother.

Worse, Oliver found a part of himself preferring the impostor. Because despite telling Frankie not to get his hopes up yesterday, Oliver had done exactly that. Deep down inside, he'd wished that finding this man would make everything okay again. That if they could somehow team up with Preston Oglethorpe to stop Mr. Kaplan, then Oliver would no longer be a chump for believing in things like heroes and families and happy endings. But one look at the sad and tattered man, and Oliver knew that such hope was just another lie. Only this time it was one he told himself.

Preston Oglethorpe approached the kids but wasn't sure whether to offer his hand or not, so he gave them each an awkward little half wave of greeting.

"Make yourselves at home, children," came a woman's voice from behind them.

"Whoa, hey!" Frankie exclaimed, wheeling around. "Who said that?"

"No need for the histrionics, young man," said Marie Curie, looking down at Frankie admonishingly from her portrait.

Frankie was dumbstruck. "You're a . . . talking picture?" he said finally.

Albert Einstein popped onto another screen. "Well, Preston, for your sake I hope this one isn't the brains of the operation."

Frankie startled again, looking at Albert with a mix of confusion and irritation.

"Don't mind him, son," Leonardo da Vinci chimed in. "He can be a bit of a jerk."

Matilda, Oliver now noticed, had taken no interest whatsoever in the talking portraits, or in Preston Oglethorpe himself. Instead, she paced slowly around the room like a detective casing a crime scene, her attention finally centering on the massive flowchart covering the far wall.

JoJo's Bar and Grill was not much to look at. A glorified shack with the structural integrity of a child's pillow fort, JoJo's sat in the middle of a gravel lot on the industrial side of town.

The inside was even less impressive. It was dark and there were germs on the floor that were probably old enough to vote.

The filth wasn't in or on JoJo's, the filth *was* JoJo's. It was probably the only thing keeping the whole place together.

The customers were a gruff, hardscrabble crowd, with lots of worn leather biker vests and chewing tobacco. Billy and Mrs. Gonzales were probably the only two people there under sixty.

It was the most interesting place Billy Fargus had ever been.

"I gotta good feeling about tonight," Bad Becky said approvingly as they made their way to the assortment of low pallets in the far corner of the room that would be the stage. "A real good feeling."

"Hey," Frankie said, pointing to Marie and Leonardo. "How come you two can speak English?"

"What part of artificial intelligence don't you understand?" Albert replied.

"One more crack out of you and I pull the plug, Einstein," Frankie said.

While Oliver and Frankie were still at the front of the warehouse, gobsmacked by talking pictures, Matilda scanned the massive flowchart on the back wall, searching for the one answer that was more important to her than all the others. A dreadful suspicion she'd tried to ignore ever since she'd first seen that old photo with Preston Oglethorpe, Oliver's mom, and her dad.

It was almost too much to take in. Countless hand-drawn boxes with arrows connecting them this way and that, each one labeled with a simple word or phrase scribbled inside. Some boxes were bigger than others. Some were crossed out. Some had multiple arrows either feeding into them or feeding out. Some were dead ends.

The chart seemed to be organized chronologically, more or less, from left to right. Matilda quickly spotted a large box labeled "CARDAMOM." Two arrows led out of that box to two other, smaller boxes that read "JAM" and "JERKY." The arrows leading out of those boxes led to other boxes, "LUNCHROOM" and "THE DOG." Matilda's eyes scanned forward to an array of other boxes, some with words she recognized but others, like "SHADY GLADES" and "JOJO'S," that she didn't.

She found boxes predicting her discovery of the black Lincolns, her fake flu, and when she'd cornered Oliver after school to warn him he was being followed. Nearly everything they'd done over the last several weeks was up there on the wall.

Now nearly anyone else in Matilda's position would be scanning ahead, following the boxes to the right to see what was going to happen next. It was, after all, the logical course of action. But right now Matilda wasn't feeling very logical. Despite all that was at stake, Matilda didn't care about the future.

She wanted to know about the past.

Matilda moved to the left, following the boxes backward in time. She found her dad's transfer to Lake Grove Glen, the previous janitor's jackpot and retirement, Oliver's dad leaving for Phoenix. Back further she went, and further still, until she found the first box, which read, inside, simply . . .

$$\boxed{\text{HIDING}}$$

Matilda stared at the box, frustrated. Then she saw a very faint, dotted line trailing from the left edge of the box. She followed the tiny, almost invisible dotted line as it extended seven or eight feet off the chart itself and down the wall to a small, plain white piece of paper taped to the wall.

"I KNEW IT!" Matilda raged from across the room.

Frankie and Oliver rushed to her side. But she could only look past them at Preston Oglethorpe, who followed the boys more slowly, his head low.

She stared at Preston Oglethorpe with a murderous look in her eyes as she pointed at the tiny scrap of paper on the wall. A piece of paper with a little box drawn on it. A box with one word inside.

DAYTON

"It was your fault, wasn't it?" Matilda demanded. Preston didn't meet her eyes, but he nodded, ever so slightly. "You absurd, pathetic, horrible man!"

"Whoa, Matilda, calm down," Frankie said.

But there was no quieting her anger. "You think this is all some kind of game, don't you?" she screamed. "Don't you?!"

Preston finally looked up, his face awash with shame and regret. "No, I don't," he said softly. "Truly, I don't."

"Oh yes, you do. You make your little charts and compute your formulas and move the rest of us around like little chess pieces."

"Matilda, what's going on?" Oliver asked.

"I know you're angry and you have every right to be," Preston said. "But I'm trying to fix things. Please, if you'll let me—"

"Oliver, we have to leave. Now," she said. Then she pointed at Preston without looking at him. "This man is dangerous."

"But you said Kaplan was dangerous."

"His name's not really Kaplan," Preston offered.

"I don't care!" Matilda cried, glaring directly at Preston now. "You nearly killed him. You have to know that."

"Matilda, I don't understand," Oliver said. "Who did he nearly kill?"

"My dad!" she said, and ran out of the warehouse.

"His name was Lester Townsend when I knew him," Preston said. "But that's not his real name, either. I'm not sure anyone else knows who he really is."

Preston and Oliver sat at the table. Alone. When Matilda had run out of the warehouse, Frankie rushed after her, stopping just at the door when he realized Oliver wasn't behind him. They shared a look. Oliver had to stay. If nothing else, he had to get some answers. For him and his mom. Someone, finally, was going to explain themselves. Frankie nodded and left.

"I first met—let's just stick with calling him 'Kaplan' for simplicity's sake, shall we?—I first met Kaplan shortly after I began my work on chaos theory. At the time, he was in charge of the government think tank that was funding my research. He became my mentor. I trusted him. I thought he was my friend. He wasn't."

Oliver knew that there was a lot going on here that he didn't understand, but Preston's feelings about George Kaplan . . . that much Oliver could relate to perfectly.

"Matilda's right, Oliver," Preston continued. "I am dangerous. Very dangerous. I can predict anything, do almost anything. I can create, destroy, manipulate, and the scariest part is that I can do it all in complete secrecy. In the wrong hands my mind could be the most powerful weapon in the history of the world."

Oliver tried to decide whether Preston referring to his mind as if it were something separate from himself was reassuring or frightening.

"What happened in Dayton?" Oliver asked.

Preston sagged in his chair, as if the question had sucked the air out of him. "Kaplan kept pushing me to test my work, to see if I could set off a complex series of events simply by manipulating one tiny element."

"The butterfly wings," Oliver said.

"Something like that," Preston said. "I agreed. Matilda's father, Jimmy, was my best friend growing up. After college he joined the FBI, so I thought, if I had to do a field test, why not one that could help his career? He was stationed in Dayton, Ohio, at the time, so I decided to test my work there. I set up a chain of events that led him to a counterfeiting ring. It should have been a routine bust, but I miscalculated. Jimmy got shot in the shoulder."

"It was an accident," Oliver offered.

"It was unforgivably foolish," Preston snapped. "Not to mention arrogant. Not only did I almost kill my best friend, but my hubris showed Kaplan the full extent of my abilities. What my math could really do. The fact that Jimmy almost died wasn't important to him. As far as he was concerned, that test was a resounding success. He left the think tank and wanted me to come with him. He went on about all the things we could do together. The money, the power—he wasn't who I thought he was."

"That's why you disappeared, then?" Oliver said. "You've been hiding from Kaplan."

"I've been hiding from everyone, Oliver," Preston said.

They sat in silence for a few moments.

Beep!

Preston took off his digital wristwatch and placed it on the table.

"What's that?" Oliver asked.

Preston looked down at his watch. "Oh, nothing."

But Oliver knew better. He was getting pretty good at spotting when an adult was lying to his face.

"Matilda!" Frankie yelled. "Wait up!"

She was halfway down the block before Frankie caught

her. And she was the kind of mad that made a person forget to breathe, so when Frankie cut her off on the sidewalk, she started taking deep, gasping breaths that quickly turned to sobs.

"Uh, there, there," Frankie said, patting her on the back uncertainly as she cried into his chest. "It's all right. There . . . there."

Eventually Matilda caught her breath and stopped crying. Then she told Frankie about her dad and how he was an FBI agent. And she told him about Dayton.

"Your dad's a Fed?" Frankie said, impressed. "Cool."

"It's not cool," Matilda insisted. "I hate it. He's already been shot once. What if it happens again? What if this time he isn't just wounded?"

"I'm sorry," Frankie said. "That really blows." Frankie thought for a minute. "That's why you're into all that spy and detective stuff, isn't it? The computer hacking, the composition book you're always writing in? You're trying to protect him."

Matilda shrugged. "Guess you think I'm a super weirdo now?"

"Nah," Frankie said. "You're still a regular weirdo."

Matilda laughed a little. They started walking, not saying much. It was a nice quiet, though.

When they reached the corner where their routes home

diverged, Frankie said, "You know, you really gotta tell your dad about all this."

"I know," Matilda said.

"I could come with you, if you want."

"That's okay," she said. Then: "Thanks, though."

He smiled. Matilda watched him turn the corner, then started on her way.

She made it about three steps before walking right into Sullivan, who scooped her up and over his shoulder before she could make a break for it.

The big man tossed her in the back seat of his black Lincoln Town Car, right next to Frankie. In the driver's seat, Gilbert turned around to give them both a "don't even think about making a sound" look.

Despite being more scared than she'd ever been in her life, the logical side of Matilda's mind suddenly wished she had peeked ahead a little further on Preston Oglethorpe's wall chart.

If Oliver had left the warehouse five minutes earlier, he might have seen his friends being captured. He might have been able to run and get help.

Or he might have been caught himself.

As it was, Oliver reached the corner where Matilda and Frankie had been snatched just moments after Gilbert and Sullivan's black Lincoln Town Car had sped away.

But even though he didn't see the kidnapping, Oliver got an uneasy feeling as he passed the corner and quickened his pace. Once he was within sight of his house, he slowed down, scouting the area warily.

Oliver watched his mom walk down the front steps with Mr. Kaplan. He ducked behind a tree but kept his eyes glued on his mom. She wasn't smiling, and Kaplan was holding her firmly by the arm.

He was taking her away.

When they reached Kaplan's car, Floss spotted Oliver across the street. Without changing her expression, she subtly mouthed the words:

RUN AWAY.

Then she got in the car with Kaplan and they drove off.

Oliver didn't know what to do. All his worst fears over the last several weeks were now coming true. He felt helpless, hopeless, and terribly alone.

Only, maybe he wasn't alone. He'd just met a man who'd know exactly where Mr. Kaplan was taking his mom. And if the picture Oliver had seen in his mom's yearbook was any indication,

Preston would care about what happened to her almost as much as Oliver did.

The only question now was could he get to Preston in time.

Bam! Oliver burst into the warehouse to find Preston sitting right where Oliver had left him.

Beep! went the wristwatch, which still sat on the table in front of Preston.

"Kaplan took my mom," Oliver said, breathless.

"I know, Oliver," Preston said flatly. "And Frankie and Matilda, too."

Oliver couldn't believe the man's emotionless reaction. He flat-out couldn't believe it. "Are you even listening to me? *Kaplan has my mom.* And you're saying he has my friends, too? Doesn't that mean anything to you?"

Preston looked at Oliver with tired, haunted eyes. "Oliver, it means everything to me," he said slowly. "But you have to trust the math."

"Trust the . . ." Oliver said, incredulous. "I can't do that. It's not my math. What you really mean is that I have to trust you. And you know what, I don't. Because you're just sitting there. You promise it's going to be okay, and then you run off to

Arizona with a Pilates instructor. Or you're nice to my mom, but it's really all a lie so you can take over the world. You guys all keep saying 'trust me,' but none of you are really who you say you are!"

"Oliver, please," Preston said. "Listen to me. I know it's hard to believe, but I've accounted for all of this. Everything that is happening now, I've factored it all in. I've already solved it."

"Solved it?" Oliver cried. "Are you crazy? You can't *solve* life! It doesn't work like that, no matter how smart you are."

Beep!

Oliver zeroed in on the digital wristwatch, unleashing what could best be likened to a war cry as he grabbed the watch off the table and smashed it back down onto the wood, pulverizing it into pieces.

Oliver ran to the door. He had to call the police, Frankie's parents, anyone who could save the people he cared about most. But as he was rushing away, he stopped, turned around, and said to Preston, "You are a worthless coward."

"I recognize this street," Frankie whispered to Matilda in the back seat. "They're taking us to the place where I tailed the one Lincoln. To Kaplan's house."

"Quiet back there," Gilbert growled from the front. As he glowered at the kids, his right hand pulsed like he was trying to squeeze something that wasn't there.

Matilda waited until the ferret-like man turned his attention back to the road. "Okay," she whispered. "When we get out, I'll distract them. Then you make a break for it."

"No way!"

"I said quiet!"

"You left your tension ball back at the house again," Sullivan said knowingly.

"Shut up, Sully."

"I'm not leaving you behind," Frankie insisted.

"It's our only move," Matilda reasoned. "You're faster and you know the area. That makes you our best shot at getting help."

Frankie knew she was right. He gave her a terse nod, then stared out the window.

They pulled into the driveway of the house. Gilbert parked around back, out of sight of the street. Sullivan opened the rear door, letting Matilda exit first.

As she climbed out, Matilda stumbled into Sullivan, wrapping him up, while Frankie dashed from the car.

"Hey!" Sullivan yelled, trying to move Matilda out of the way to grab Frankie. Matilda stomped hard on Sullivan's toe, causing him to yell "Hey!" again.

Gilbert was out of the car by now, but Frankie had already darted down the driveway.

"Take the girl inside," Gilbert growled at Sullivan. "I'll get the brat."

Frankie made it about a block or so before Gilbert peeled out of the driveway after him. With the Lincoln gaining fast, Frankie knew he had to get off the street, so he ran between two houses and hopped a fence into a yard with a large tree. He climbed up about halfway, giving him a decent overhead view of the area.

Gilbert, unfortunately, was no fool and began circling the block slowly, like a shark. Frankie knew he couldn't wait him out, not with Matilda in danger back at Kaplan's. It was up to him to save her.

The best he could do was time his move and make another run for it.

Sullivan, his pride and his foot both bruised, dragged Matilda into the house. Kaplan sat in the living room with a woman who very clearly did not want to be sitting with him. Matilda surmised that this must be Oliver's mom.

Giving George Kaplan only a cursory glance, Matilda jerked her arm free from Sullivan's grip and walked over to Floss.

"I'm friends with Oliver," she said, extending her hand. "My name is Matilda Sandoval."

"Sandoval?" Floss said, shaking her head. "You wouldn't be . . ."

"That's right," Matilda said. "You and my dad went to school together."

"Jimmy?" Floss said, trying to make sense of it all. "Jimmy Sandoval is your dad?"

Matilda nodded, then threw a dismissive glance toward Kaplan. "Has he told you what this is all about?"

"He said something about trying to find Preston Oglethorpe," Floss said. "I tried to tell him that Preston left town when we were kids and never came back."

"Actually," Matilda said, "he's been back in town for a while, working as the janitor at our school."

George Kaplan's eyes lit up with glee. "Capital!" he exclaimed. "And you've seen him?"

"About half an hour ago," Matilda said. "But I wouldn't count my chickens just yet, pal."

"Oh, no?" Kaplan chuckled. "Do enlighten me, young lady, as to why I may be celebrating prematurely."

"Because Preston Oglethorpe is certifiably insane."

There was absolute silence for a moment, as if the gravity of Matilda's statement had sucked all the air from the room.

And then George Kaplan laughed.

"I'm serious," Matilda said. "We're talking antisocial personality disorder, social anxiety, paranoia—"

"Oh, I do appreciate the clinical diagnosis, my dear," he said patronizingly. "But you just let me worry about Preston Oglethorpe's state of mind."

"You're not listening to me," Matilda said impatiently. "Look, I get that you want to use him as some kind of weapon for world domination, but it won't work. The man can't control his own mind. So what makes you think you can control him?"

Kaplan took her measure. "Because I happen to know the only thing in the world that Preston Oglethorpe doesn't."

"Really? And what's that?"

"I know Preston Oglethorpe."

Preston paced back and forth in the warehouse muttering to himself.

"Trust the math, trust the math, trust the math . . ."

His eyes locked on the flowchart, the boxes and arrows that had gotten it all right up to now. The numbers hadn't let him down yet.

"Trust the math," he said again, trying to make it stick.

Preston looked over at the portraits, but they had all gone dark.

He was on his own.

The equation would work. In his head he had no doubt. But . . .

"AAARRGGGH!" Preston cried, clamping his hands on either side of his head as if he could physically contain all his thoughts. Then he ran to the nearest computer station and started typing furiously. The screens lit up with various images, maps of the city, satellite imagery of the area, traffic light grid schedules, anything and everything that was happening on every street in a three-mile radius.

Preston absorbed it all, then closed his eyes tightly.

And committed all of it to memory.

CHAPTER ELEVEN

Fast and Furious: Chicagoland Drift * That Many Names
Is Never a Good Sign * They Say Most Accidents Occur
within Five Miles of the Home * Did Anyone Hear That? *
Best to Perhaps Look Away * The Steepest Hill in Illinois *
Jimmy Gets a Sign * Down Goes Beecham * Well,
That Didn't Take Long

Oliver stood at the corner, wondering which way to go. Everyone he cared about was in danger, and he didn't know who to turn to.

An old Oldsmobile Cutlass jerked to a stop on the curb, facing the wrong way on the street.

"Oliver! Get in!"

Oliver looked over at Preston, leaning awkwardly out the window.

"Please," Preston said.

"Why?" Oliver said.

"Because you were right. About everything. And I need your help."

Oliver got in the car.

"Okay," Preston said. "Where's Kaplan holing up?"

"What?" Oliver exclaimed, fastening his seat belt. "How can you not know that?"

"Because I didn't need to. Frankie found it last week, didn't he?"

"Um, yeah," Oliver said, warily conceding the logical absurdity of his point. "A bungalow at 714 Euclid."

Preston nodded but then, curiously, did nothing. He just sat there, mumbling numbers and equations to himself with his eyes closed.

"What are you doing?" Oliver asked.

"Quiet," Preston squeezed in amid the mumbling. "Please." He then opened his eyes and stared fixedly up the street. "Three, two," he said softly. "One."

Then Preston peeled off down the street, driving fast with one hand while the other kept a kind of metronome time on the dashboard.

"Where are you going?" Oliver asked, confused.

"To 714 Euclid," Preston said between counts on the dash. "Like you said."

"But that's the other way."

"Oliver, how familiar are you with non-Euclidean geometry?"

"Not terribly."

Preston gave Oliver a momentary glance as he swerved suddenly to avoid an oncoming car. "Well, I tell you what. We survive the afternoon, and I'd be more than happy to give you a crash course."

Oliver was willing to look past Preston's sarcasm, but at this particular moment he really wished the man had avoided saying the word "crash."

Jimmy Sandoval was driving up Interstate 94, about five miles from the Wisconsin border, when his cell phone lit up with an emergency alert from the FBI criminal database.

"What the . . ." Matilda's father muttered, pulling over at the next exit. When he clicked on the alert, his screen filled with the results of a facial recognition match.

Suddenly Jimmy was looking at a surveillance photo of a handsome, dashing-looking man.

Jimmy had no idea who this man was. Neither, it appeared, did the FBI. The man had more aliases than most people have socks.

Victor Larrabee

Lester Townsend

George Kaplan

The list of assumed names went on. Jimmy tried to access the rest of the file but was blocked by the server; whoever this guy was, Matilda's dad didn't have the clearance to know anything more about him.

Confused, Jimmy brought up the facial recognition request he had apparently made to the criminal database last night. Sure enough, his computer had sent a driver's license photo of this guy under the presumed name of George Kaplan.

"I didn't take this. So who did?" Jimmy stared at the picture, confused.

Then not so confused.

"Matilda."

Jimmy dropped his phone, got back on the highway, and high-tailed it back toward Chicago.

Meanwhile, Frankie and Gilbert were still playing cat-and-mouse across the neighborhood. Frankie cut across the streets when he had to but tried to keep to the backyards as much as possible.

He was running out of neighborhood to work with, however. Though the area was still residential, if he was going to get help, he was going to have to cross a patch of longer, wider commercial streets.

Frankie peeked out from behind the fence he was using for cover. The coast seemed clear, but once he made a run for it, he'd have to go at least a couple hundred yards before he could hide again. And, man, was he tired.

Summoning the last of his energy, Frankie bolted from behind the fence and sprinted down the street.

A few blocks away, Gilbert's Lincoln Town Car eased slowly out of its own hiding place, toying with Frankie as it quietly gained on him.

By the time Frankie realized that Gilbert was closing in, he was too exhausted to make another break for it. He kept running but knew it was only a matter of time before he was done for.

Frankie reached an intersection at the bottom of a steep hill, his lungs on fire and his legs throbbing with pain. The Town Car was only half a block away now but gaining slowly and taunting him with its patience. Frankie could even see Gilbert laughing cruelly inside the car.

What Frankie couldn't see was that way, way up at the top of that hill was . . .

That old Cadillac. The one he and Archie passed every day on their walks.

Now, the lone tire block holding the car in place at the top of the hill was heavy enough. But Archie had one hard head. And days upon weeks of banging that head into the block had, little by little, nudged it out of place. In fact, the tire block was now only barely holding the rear tire in check. The tiniest disruption would cause the car to break free entirely.

Like, say, the timed lawn sprinklers three houses up the block. In particular, the busted sprinkler head closest to the curb, which dribbled a steady stream of water that rivered down the gutters, carrying just enough current to nudge the tire block that last little bit, allowing the Cadillac's back tire to rotate, ever so slowly, forward.

Back down at the bottom of the hill, Frankie doubled over in exhaustion. He looked at the Town Car and waited for Gilbert to get out and capture him again.

Except Gilbert didn't do that. He didn't get out of the car. Instead he gunned the engine and started driving straight for Frankie.

Knowing he didn't have the time or strength to dodge the car, Frankie accepted his fate. He stood up straight and closed his eyes in defiant bravery.

And completely missed the beautiful moment when

the runaway Cadillac rolled down the hill and pulverized Gilbert's car less than a foot away from where Frankie was standing.

Frankie opened his eyes in shock as he surveyed the glorious carnage all around him.

"Judas Priest!" He laughed.

It was a great moment, though sadly one that didn't last long. Gilbert—battered, bloody, and bruised—crawled out of the car and glared at Frankie with a murderous rage.

"Aw, come on," Frankie said.

The Dangerous Jams ended their set on a really killer number. And the gig was a smashing success—literally. At JoJo's, a gig wasn't a hit unless someone threw at least one chair into a wall. The whole bar had been rocking. It was wild, loud, and thoroughly awesome. At one point, Billy thought he heard a car crash outside, but no one bothered to check.

Shortly after the gig, though, Mrs. Gonzales came up to Billy and Bad Becky to tell them that she was taking Mr. Abernale and Mr. Lindo back to Shady Glades.

"This sort of thing takes a lot out of Mr. Lindo," she said. "Billy, I've spoken with your mom, and she'll be here to pick you up soon. Ms. Tillman, I can send the shuttle van for you later, if you like."

"That's all right, ma'am," Bad Becky said dismissively. "One of these clowns will get me home."

The car was going to crash. It hadn't happened yet, but Oliver knew it was inevitable. It had to. Because Preston was racing through the city streets with absolute focus but no obvious purpose. Sometimes he slowed down for no reason, other times he sped up, running stop signs and red lights without a second glance, only to then come to a screeching stop in the middle of the street. He changed direction constantly, a few times against traffic. Oliver wasn't sure if Preston was insane or just didn't know how to drive or both.

At the moment, Preston was running yet another red light just as a very fast-moving delivery truck barreled into the intersection, where it would no doubt T-bone them viciously.

Instead, the truck seamlessly made a right-hand turn, missing their car completely.

The color drained from Oliver's face.

"It might be easier," Preston said calmly, "if you closed your eyes."

"I'd love to, but I can't." Oliver's body was rigid, his eyes fixed forward, too terrified to even blink. He was literally scared stiff.

Preston took a hard turn into an alley and gunned the engine. Then he turned to Oliver, giving the boy his full attention. "Before we get to Kaplan's, I need you to understand something—"

"Don't look at me!" Oliver cried. "Look at the road!"

"I don't have to look at the road," Preston said reasonably as a dog walker passed in front of them with less than a second to spare. "I only need to maintain the course at a constant speed and—"

"JUST LOOK AT THE ROAD!"

"Very well." Preston sighed. "But this might be my only chance to apologize."

"First things first," Oliver said. "Get my mom back, then you can apologize."

Preston cocked his head. "Quite right," he said.

This had to be the steepest hill in the Midwest, or at least it felt like that to Frankie. Not even the adrenaline-fueled fear of looking back and seeing Gilbert limping after him with determination like a murder-crazed cyborg could quicken Frankie's pace. Sprinting up the hill felt like running in a dream, exhausting and fruitless.

His legs were jelly and he'd nearly passed out from light-headedness when he heard the music. Raucous, head-banging music. Frankie found a renewed energy as he clumsily lumbered toward that music. It was amazing what a person could do when they had a soundtrack to spur them on.

But it wasn't enough. Gilbert finally caught Frankie right outside a biker bar, grabbing him by the neck and sneering into the boy's face. The henchman's neck veins bulged, and steaming fury snarled from his nostrils.

"You're done for now, boy."

For the second time in less than ten minutes, Frankie closed his eyes and awaited his death.

"Hey! Chicken pesto on olive!"

Frankie opened his eyes to find Billy Fargus standing in the doorway of the biker bar. He slurped a Coke and watched Frankie's impending murder with a look Frankie wished was full of a lot more alarm and a little less idle curiosity.

"Yeah, that *is* you. Man, that was some sandwich," Billy said with respect. Then, almost as an afterthought: "Is this guy bothering you?"

"Beat it, punk," Gilbert growled.

Billy just smiled, because while the ferret-faced dude shook

Frankie down, Bad Becky and two dozen old warhorses had come out to see what was going on.

"Pick up, pick up!" Jimmy yelled at his phone as he sped down the street.

There was no answer at home. He tried Matilda's cell again. Again nothing.

Jimmy nearly ran a red light, slamming on the brakes just before the intersection. He gripped the steering wheel with both hands, fear and adrenaline nearly ripping it off the shaft.

Then, just before the light changed, a group of bikers raced across the intersection. On the back of one bike was a boy about his daughter's age.

On the back of another bike was another, bigger boy, also about Matilda's age.

On the back of a third bike was a wiry, mean-looking man in an ill-fitting business suit, gagged and hog-tied to the seat.

But what really caught Jimmy's attention was the club name on the back of all the bikers' jackets.

THE ANGRY CLOWNS.

This was, by far, the coolest Frankie had ever felt in his entire life. Riding on the back of a motorcycle, wind in his face, the deep rumble and shake of the motorcycle's engine numbing his butt, not to mention the smell of sweaty, old leather. It was just awesome.

As the geriatric motorcycle club passed Henry's Market, Frankie glimpsed the owner, Henry Beecham, standing out front. A man and a woman with briefcases and expensive suits waited patiently while Mr. Beecham finished reading a bound stack of papers.

The beastly engine under Frankie roared, pulling his attention back to the road ahead. But just before he looked away, the woman handed Mr. Beecham a check. Mr. Beecham took one look at it and smiled broadly.

And then promptly collapsed to the ground.

Preston parked his car down the block from George Kaplan's house. The sun had slipped below the horizon line, and the last light of dusk softly faded into darkness.

"What do we do now?" Oliver asked.

Preston, lost in thought, didn't seem to hear him.

Oliver started to ask again but was distracted by a tap on the window.

Sullivan, gun in hand, pressed his face against Oliver's window. "Mr. Kaplan's been expecting you," he said through the glass.

The big man glanced at Preston. The scrawny little guy didn't look like much, but Sully remembered his boss's description of Oglethorpe's abilities and shuddered. Then he looked up to the sky, half expecting a giant plastic Mouse Trap net to fall on top of him.

CHAPTER TWELVE

Awkward Introductions ✳ Preston Oglethorpe Stops Thinking

Approximately two and a half minutes after Sullivan led Preston and Oliver away at gunpoint, Frankie, Billy, Bad Becky, and the Angry Clowns pulled up behind Preston's recently abandoned car.

About forty-five seconds after *that*, they were joined by Jimmy Sandoval, who came to a screeching halt just behind the caravan of motorcycles.

"Special Agent James Sandoval," he said, flashing his badge, a mixture of stern authority and parental panic on his face.

"Aw, man," groaned a hulking, bearded Angry Clown. "It's the fuzz."

Frankie stepped to the front of the group. "No worries, Mad Dog. I got this."

"Hey, I recognize you!" Matilda's dad said, pointing a suspicious finger at Frankie. "You were on my front porch!"

Frankie turned back to Mad Dog and the others. "This might take a minute."

What followed was a brief but tense conversation. Frankie admitted the bare bones of what he, Matilda, and Oliver had been up to the last couple of months, and Jimmy explained that finding Preston Oglethorpe was the reason the Sandovals had moved to town. Mr. Sandoval looked like a responsible adult, so Frankie knew there'd be an inevitable call to his parents. But for now, they were both after the same thing: saving Matilda and Preston. Which is how Frankie found himself on a garage roof, scouting Kaplan's house with a borrowed pair of binoculars.

"When's backup getting here?" Frankie asked. "I figure SWAT can set up over there, across the street." He passed the binoculars to Matilda's father.

"No backup," Jimmy said. "This needs to happen as quietly as possible."

"What?"

"Can't risk the exposure," Jimmy said. "Whoever this George Kaplan guy is, he isn't the only bad guy out there who'd like to get his hands on Preston Oglethorpe."

Frankie looked over the edge of the garage to the alley below,

201

where Billy and the Angry Clowns were tormenting the hog-tied and helpless Gilbert.

"Um," Frankie said, "should we be doing something about that?"

Jimmy glanced down. "No time," he said. He closed the binoculars and scooted to the edge of the roof.

"What are we gonna do?" Frankie asked.

"*We* aren't going to do anything," Matilda's dad said, flicking his legs over the gutter and shimmying down a drainpipe. "*I* am going in through the front door."

"Really?" Frankie called down after him. "That's all you got?"

"The gang is all here." George Kaplan clapped his hands in delight as Sullivan led Preston and Oliver into the living room. "You look well, Preston."

Oliver glanced across the room at Matilda, then ran to his mother. She held him protectively as she stared in disbelief at the man she hadn't seen in over twenty years.

"Preston?" she said. "Is that you?"

Preston barely looked at her, his expression unreadable. "Hello, Floss," he said quietly.

"You really are back."

"For several months now," Kaplan interjected. "Shortly after your husband split, in fact. I think Preston wanted to be there for you in your time of emotional need. But it's so hard to coax him out from behind his equations. Isn't it, Preston?" Kaplan gave him a "there, there" pat on the shoulder.

"So you spied on us," Oliver said, stepping between his mother and Kaplan. "Lied to us. Pretended to be someone else. This was all a trap to catch Preston, wasn't it?"

"No, no, Oliver. You've got it all wrong, dear boy. *Catch* Preston Oglethorpe? I doubt such a thing is even possible."

"Then why did you do it?" Matilda jumped in. "If you weren't trying to catch him, why all the role-playing? Why all the games?"

Oliver had been wondering the same thing, but looking at the smug smirk on George Kaplan's face, it suddenly all made sense. "You never wanted to capture him," he said. "You wanted to break him. That's what all this was about. You were living the life Preston wanted and rubbing his nose in it."

"I must say, that's a rather vicious way of looking at it, Oliver," Kaplan replied. "I merely needed to show our dear Preston where he belongs."

"With you?" Matilda said with contempt.

"Precisely. With me."

"So you can control him!"

"So I can protect him," George Kaplan corrected. "He can't

function out here, in the world. Surely even you children can see that now." He turned his attention to Preston and said softly, "Can't you see it, too, Preston?"

Preston looked away, his entire posture one of sadness and defeat.

"Don't listen to him," Oliver said.

"But he's right," Preston said. "You said so yourself. I'm worthless."

"I was wrong. He is wrong," Oliver insisted. "Besides. Don't let him, or me, or anyone tell you who you are."

Preston looked at Oliver quizzically, the words striking a chord.

"Oh, Oliver, you have such spark." Kaplan was impressed. "After college, I do hope you'll come to me for employment. In the meantime, however, I wouldn't fret too much about all of this. It's like we talked about. People generally have no idea what they really want, much less what they need. They just think they do. But with Preston I can fix all that. I can run the entire world, put everything in its proper place, and no one will ever even know."

"But it would all be a lie," Oliver said.

"Oh, don't begrudge a good lie, Oliver. Most people can't get through the day without one."

Oliver clenched his teeth and did something totally out of character. He got right in Kaplan's face. "You're not taking him."

"Oliver, don't you see?" George Kaplan said patiently. "I'm doing this *for* him. Preston needs the world bottled for him. When it springs straight from the tap, it's just too much."

Oliver looked over at Preston, who couldn't meet the boy's eyes.

"Even Preston knows it now," Kaplan continued. "Honestly, son. He's been in love with your mother since they were kids. She was his muse. His life's work was built on a little boy's dream to give that girl the perfect day." He gestured to Oliver's mom. "It's staggering, really. All that genius, but even now he can barely look at her." George Kaplan lifted Preston's chin with his finger. "Go on, now, Preston. Look at her."

Preston did, and just like that fateful evening on Floss's front porch, his mind froze. Once again he became that confused, strange little boy standing dumbly with an immobile, catatonic look on his face as a random accident and an angry clown ruined his big shot at love.

"See?" George Kaplan sneered. "He can't go after what he wants. He simply can't."

"Stop it!" Oliver cried.

"And the cruelest irony of all is that this entire time, Preston, I think she may have loved you back."

"I said leave him alone!"

"A few weeks, Preston. That's all the time I needed to make your dreams my reality. You've had a lifetime to make her feel that way, and you failed. Because you just don't understand what people want. What they need. And you never will. This isn't the life for you. Your life is the mind."

Kaplan patted Preston on the shoulder again, this time leaving his hand there as a comforting but, more importantly, controlling gesture.

Floss jumped from her seat and charged at Kaplan, but Sullivan held her back. And even though Preston could hear her calling his name, trying to get his attention, it all sounded so very far away. Everyone sounded so very far away.

Until Oliver's voice cut through the din with the last three words Preston ever expected.

"Farouk's Famous Fudgsicles."

"Come again?" Kaplan snickered.

"I said," Oliver repeated, "Farouk's Famous Fudgsicles."

Preston stared at Oliver in gobsmacked wonder. "How do you even know what those are? They stopped making them almost twenty years ago."

"Because my mom saved an old Fudgsicle stick with that printed on one side. Kept it taped to the back of an old yearbook. You know what it said on the other side?"

Preston shook his head; it was a not a gesture his neck muscles were used to making.

"On the other side," Oliver continued, "it said: 'my perfect day.' Now, I may not be some super genius or a criminal master-mind, but I can connect a dot or two. So while I don't know what made that day so perfect, I'm pretty sure you had something to do with it. And not because of math or physics or formulas, but because of *you*. Because you were her friend. That's all. Don't you see, Preston? It's not about numbers or variables or solutions, and it's sure not about perfection. Sometimes it's just about a Fudgsicle."

For a moment, there was nothing. Not a sound. Then George Kaplan started slowly clapping. "Bravo, Oliver!" Kaplan said. "That was truly moving. Inspiring, even. But I'm afraid, in the final tally, that it's just not enough." He turned to face Preston, looking him squarely, commandingly, in the eye. "Am I right, Preston?"

It was then that Preston Oglethorpe, for perhaps the first time in his life, did something completely spontaneous. Completely impulsive and uncalculated. No equations, no boxes, no math. In fact, Preston Oglethorpe didn't think at all.

He just wheeled back and punched George Kaplan square in the nose.

What came next seemed to happen in slow motion.

Sullivan drew his gun as Kaplan staggered back, catching himself on the table . . . where Gilbert had left his tension ball.

The jostled ball began to slowly roll across the table, until it bumped into a large takeout box of shrimp lo mein that was balanced precariously on the table's edge, knocking it over.

The takeout box fell into the trash can below, which tipped over, spilling a half-full Big Gulp across the floor.

"And just what are you smiling about?!" Kaplan yelled at Preston, who, despite cradling his throbbing punching hand, did indeed have a rather goofy smile on his face.

By this time the spilled soda had reached a nearby tangle of loose electrical cords, causing them to spark and smoke.

Sullivan clumsily sprang to action, dropping his gun and nudging the nearby desk's rolling swivel chair into his boss on the way to the fire extinguisher.

Kaplan snatched up the gun. "Watch it, you buffoon!" he screamed at Sullivan as he kicked the rolling chair back across the room.

The chair spun like a top through a half-open bedroom door, pushing it open to reveal the sliding closet mirrors along the back wall.

And that enabled Kaplan to spot Jimmy Sandoval's reflection as he slipped inside the front door. But Kaplan, more accustomed to giving orders than taking action himself, panicked and shot at the reflection in the mirror and not at the federal agent currently behind him.

The bullet missed the mirror and hit the doorframe,

ricocheting back toward Jimmy just as Preston ever so gently pushed him to the side . . .

. . . taking the bullet himself.

Okay, so maybe Preston Oglethorpe had thought a *little*.

"Drop the gun!" Jimmy yelled, pointing his weapon at Kaplan and Sullivan. "Both of you, on the ground, now!"

Jimmy handcuffed the would-be supervillain and his buffoonish henchman. He looked up at Matilda, registering the shock and fear on her face.

"Sandoval!" Jimmy said, getting her attention. "Status."

Matilda snapped to. "Clear!" she said. "Two hostiles on premises secured. One off-site, whereabouts unknown."

Relieved, Jimmy said, more softly this time: "Civilians?"

"We're fine, Daddy," Matilda said. "But . . ."

Jimmy followed her gaze to Preston, who was propped up against the wall with a fresh bullet wound in his shoulder.

Jimmy and Floss rushed to Preston's side. Preston's eyes darted between his two friends and finally came to rest on Oliver, a boy who had, if maybe only for a moment, made him believe that he was more than the numbers in his head. A look that could best be described as contented—bemused, even—settled on Preston's face.

"Thank you," he said . . . and then passed out.

CHAPTER THIRTEEN

Oliver and Floss hopped into the ambulance so they could ride
to the hospital with Preston just as George Kaplan, Gilbert, and
Sullivan were dragged away by men in dark suits and dark sun-
glasses. Shortly after that, Frankie's parents arrived on the scene.

As stressful and taxing as the day had been, it was the following twenty minutes that drained Matilda the most. Everyone,
from her dad to Frankie's parents to Billy Fargus and a geriatric
motorcycle gang, not to mention a dozen paramedics and federal
agents, crowded around Matilda looking for answers.

She seemed to be the only one who could explain what she,

Oliver, and Frankie had done the last few weeks, how she came to suspect George Kaplan was not who he'd said he was, and how *that* led them to discover that their janitor was, in fact, the smartest person in the world, and how *that* led them to being kidnapped and held hostage in a lovely little bungalow in the garden district. When she said it all out loud, it didn't sound like a huge deal.

But Matilda doubted her dad would see it the same way.

"Do you realize what you've done?" he asked, once they were in the car and alone. "You've hacked into several government databases and electronically impersonated a federal agent to look at highly classified files while at the same time withholding critical information in an ongoing FBI investigation with national security implications." Jimmy Sandoval fixed his daughter with a serious look. The kind that meant she was, at the very least, indefinitely grounded.

"You *lied* to me," Matilda said simply.

Jimmy opened his mouth to respond. Then he closed it and considered for a moment.

"Call it even?"

"Deal."

"Good," Jimmy said, starting the car. "Now, what in the world are we going to tell your mother?"

Oliver sat in the back of the ambulance as it raced across town, sirens blaring. He knew there were a lot of things he should be feeling right now, but the truth of it was that Oliver felt surprisingly numb. Like he wasn't even there, really. At the same time, he had a nagging sense that this feeling would soon wear off in a sudden and unwelcome way. Like when you know your leg has fallen asleep and when you finally try to move it's going to feel like a million tiny needles stabbing all at once.

His mom sat up near the front with Preston, who was awake now and laid out on a stretcher.

"So," she began, "your brain is a national security asset, and you've been hiding out as a middle school janitor and spying on my son for the last two and a half months?"

"Yes," Preston said.

"And is it true what Kaplan said about how you feel about me?"

"Yes," Preston said.

Oliver's mom didn't smile or gush, but she didn't look angry, either. "Why didn't you ever say anything?"

Preston swallowed and bit his lip a little before answering.

"I couldn't get the numbers to work."

"I may not be the smartest man in the world," Matilda's dad said with a self-effacing shrug, "but when Preston disappeared so soon after the botched raid in Dayton, well, let's just say I had a hunch."

Matilda smiled. Despite all the danger, the fear, the moments when it looked like all hope was lost, it had turned out to be a pretty good day. Preston was out of surgery and in stable condition, George Kaplan and his goons were in federal custody, and, to Matilda's considerable relief, she was not.

Instead, she sat in a hospital waiting room, talking with her dad.

Jimmy went on to explain how Preston's disappearance caused a full-blown panic attack in the scientific and intelligence communities. As Preston's oldest and dearest friend, he'd been put in charge of trying to find him. Hence the family's sudden move to Lake Grove Glen, Jimmy and Preston's hometown.

"Where you could keep an eye on Oliver's mom," Matilda reasoned.

"Well, that was the plan," Jimmy said. "In fact, I was putting together a massive surveillance and protection detail for Oliver and his mom. A round-the-clock team of agents, all the best spy tech—they were even giving me a dedicated satellite. We were all set to go." Matilda's dad scratched the back of his head and sighed. "We were supposed to start first thing tomorrow."

"No way!" Matilda laughed.

"Right? Talk about rotten timing. But the thing was, ever since we got into town, I kept getting sidetracked." Matilda's dad shook his head ruefully. "Every week or so, I'd get a new tip that one of Kaplan's men had been spotted in Toledo or used a credit card in Indianapolis. Or Detroit. Or Milwaukee."

"So all those trips you were taking, that was really just Kaplan leading you on a wild-goose chase?" Matilda asked. "He knew you were still flying solo, so he kept luring you out of town to distract you and slow you down."

"Well, I hate to say it, but it worked. I didn't even know you and Oliver had become friends." He shook his head. "Doesn't make me look too good as an agent or a parent, does it?"

"Don't be so hard on yourself," Matilda said. "It's a pretty big school, and I'm not the most socially gifted twelve-year-old. There's no way you could have guessed Oliver and I would even meet."

Imagine the odds, she thought with a smile.

That night, Oliver sat in his room, video chatting with Matilda and Frankie.

"It's an alphabet soup of dark suits downstairs in my living room," Matilda quipped from her bedroom. "FBI, NSA, CIA, DOD. I think there's even a FEMA guy here for some reason. Total chaos."

"Yeah, my mom's downstairs giving her statement to a couple of your dad's guys," Oliver said.

"It's crazy here, too," Frankie said. "But that's mostly just the twins."

"You guys okay, though?" Oliver said. "I mean, really?"

"We're fine, Oliver," Matilda said.

"Thanks to you, buddy," Frankie chimed in.

"No doubt," Matilda said. "You were very brave."

"I wasn't the one who got kidnapped," Oliver said. "That must have been scary."

"I may have peed a little," Frankie said. "Couple of drops. Once or twice."

"Gross, Frankie!" Matilda scolded.

Oliver laughed. And that's when all the things he'd been holding inside finally hit him. Not just the events of the day, but everything from the last few weeks. And the months before that. His parents splitting up, his dad leaving, his mom struggling to make it all work by herself.

All of it.

But mostly, it was the pretending. Pretending he didn't know that Kaplan was evil. Pretending that he didn't see how sad his mom had been since his dad left. Pretending he didn't know about Belchertown. Pretending that he didn't miss his dad. Pretending that his dad missed him.

"Guys," he said. "I gotta go."

Oliver closed his computer, curled up on his bed, and let it all out. The expression "a good cry" never made much sense to him before. But it kinda did now.

Half an hour later, he heard the agents who had been interviewing his mom leave, and he went downstairs.

"Hey, sport," his mom said softly. "I didn't know you were still up."

Oliver shrugged. His mother took in his blotchy face and came to him, wrapping him up in her arms.

Oliver had thought he was done crying. He was mistaken.

"I'm so sorry, Oliver," his mom said tearily. "I let that man in our house, I—"

"No, Mom," Oliver said, pulling away just enough to look at her. "It's not your fault. I let him in, too."

"It's my job to protect you," his mom said.

"It's my job to protect *you*," Oliver responded.

Oliver's mom looked at him, and for the first time in a long while, really saw him.

"So it is," she said.

A week later, Floss sat at a table in the hospital cafeteria, drinking coffee. She'd been coming to see Preston every day, an hour here, an hour there. It surprised her how quickly, once she got her head around what Preston's life had been these last years, they'd fallen back into their old ways. How all the genius stuff just went away and he was her oldest and best friend again.

Across the room, Floss saw an older man in a hospital gown steeping his tea at the condiments counter. He struggled when it came time to put the lid on the cup, unable to find the sweet spot.

Floss considered going to help him. He seemed like a nice man. But then, so had George Kaplan. So had her ex-husband. Everyone *seemed* nice, but how could you know? After everything that she and Oliver had been through, wasn't it easier, and safer, to just put up walls?

But she didn't want to become that person. More importantly, she didn't want Oliver to become that person. Even before this nightmare with Kaplan, or whoever he really was, she could see in her son's eyes that he was starting to view the world around him with suspicion and distrust. And even though those eyes couldn't see her now, Floss wanted to show him that who we are is the sum of the tiny, random choices we make every day. It all adds up.

"Can I help with you that?" she asked the man.

"Guys, I'm home!"

Matilda ran down the stairs to find her dad standing in the doorway with pizza and soda. Her heart sank in her chest.

They were moving again. After all they'd been through, and just when things were getting good.

Matilda wasn't a crier, but this time she couldn't help it.

Her mom came in from the kitchen and looked at Jimmy, who shrugged helplessly.

"What? Matilda, honey. What's wrong?"

"We're moving again."

"What?" her dad said. "No, we're not."

"Yes, we are. Whenever you come home with surprise pizza, it's always because you got a new assignment, and then we move to a new city."

Her dad looked to her mom, who shrugged as if to say, "She's not wrong." He put the food on the table and went to Matilda.

"I'm sorry, honey," he said. "I didn't—" He stopped himself. "I'm sorry," he said.

Matilda nodded.

"But," he said. "We're really not moving this time."

Matilda looked up. "We're not?"

"Nope," he said. "I did get a new assignment. Well, sort of. Now instead of trying to find Preston Oglethorpe, I'm in charge of protecting him."

"I don't understand."

"Well, George Kaplan won't be the last person who'll want to poach Preston. Someone's got to keep an eye on him."

"We get to stay?"

"We get to stay."

Matilda started crying again, but this time they were tears of relief. And for the first time in a long time, Matilda felt hungry for pizza.

Later that night, when she was getting ready for bed, her mom knocked on the door.

"Honey," her mom said. "You got a minute?"

"Sure, Mom."

Her mother came in holding a thin box roughly two feet by three feet. "Here. I got you a little something."

Matilda opened the gift and pulled out a framed print. It was a portrait of a beautiful woman with long black hair and piercing eyes against a background of blueprint schematics, her head surrounded by various equations, graphing functions, and equipment designs.

"That's Hedy Lamarr," her mom explained. "She was a huge movie star back in the 1930s. But she was also a scientist and an inventor. In fact, she co-invented a communication system that allowed radio signals to rapidly hop frequency. That technology led to cell phones, GPS, and Bluetooth."

"Wow," Matilda said. "I'm a little embarrassed I've never heard of her."

"Well, you have now." Her mom smiled.

Matilda took the *Moonglow* poster off the wall and put up the portrait in its place.

"Thanks, Mom," she said.

"Our rotten luck," Frankie said, nudging Oliver in the arm. "Now we'll never get rid of her."

Matilda had just told the boys about her dad's new assignment and how it meant she'd be sticking around for a while.

"I'm happy for you, Matilda," Oliver said, forcing a smile. "I really am."

Matilda gave him a funny look. "What do you mean?" Then it clicked. "Oh, Oliver. I forgot. I'm so sorry."

"What?" Frankie said. "I'm not following." He looked at Oliver for help. Then it came to him. "Crud. Belchertown."

It had been weighing on Oliver for the last couple of days. Once the excitement of Kaplan's arrest had worn off, he remembered all the other worries he'd put aside these last several weeks. Like how he and his mom were going to have to sell the house and move to Massachusetts.

No George Kaplan meant no job for his mom, even if it hadn't been a real job in the first place. So now, despite finding the smartest man in the world and stopping an evil villain bent on world domination, it looked like Oliver and his mom were still right back where they had been at the start of the school year.

Frankie summed it up perfectly.

Crud.

When Oliver got home, he heard his mom on the phone.

"Yes, Mr. Beecham," his mom was saying. "Sorry, sorry. *Henry.*"

Oliver wandered into the living room. Mrs. Figge sat on the couch while Oliver's mom paced around the room as she talked.

"Well, thank you. Of course, that sounds great."

Oliver gave Frankie's mom a questioning look. She shrugged.

"Are you serious?" his mom said. "No, no, that's more than generous. Absolutely! See you Monday."

Floss hung up the phone. Her eyes were teary, but they looked like happy tears this time.

"I got a job!"

Mrs. Figge jumped up and the two women hugged.

"Here?" Oliver said.

"Here!" his mom said.

"So, no Belchertown?"

"Nope," Floss said. "No Belchertown— Wait, how did you know? You know what, never mind. No Belchertown, and no selling the house!"

Oliver felt like a great weight had been lifted off his shoulders. He couldn't wait to tell Frankie and Matilda.

"Oh my God," Mrs. Figge said, overjoyed. "But how did this happen?"

"You know Henry Beecham? He owns that market over on MacDonald. Well, he makes this gourmet jam that is kind of a big deal. He just got an offer to distribute it nationally. And he needs someone to run his marketing."

"When did this all come about?" Mrs. Figge asked, perplexed. "Did you interview for this?"

"I didn't." Oliver's mom laughed. "Not really. I just bumped into him one day at the hospital—I was there visiting Preston—and we talked and, I don't know, it just happened."

"Wow," Mrs. Figge said. "I mean, imagine the odds!"

Oliver's face clouded over. He should have been happy, but one mention of Preston, followed closely by "odds," instantly soured his mood.

Suddenly, he just wanted to be alone.

"Wanna go to the hospital after school?" Matilda said the next day.

"No. No, thanks."

She and Oliver were sitting in the bleachers during gym class.

The class was playing dodgeball, and Frankie was still in the game. He had kind of become the king of gym dodgeball. All that running with Archie was really paying off. He could run circles around everyone else, and his reflexes were faster, too.

"Preston gets out tomorrow, you know," Matilda said. "Kinda harsh if you don't visit him at least once."

Oliver shrugged. Maybe he wanted to be harsh.

"Look, I know this isn't really my business," Matilda said. "But I thought you sort of liked Preston."

"I don't know. He's fine, I guess," Oliver said. "That doesn't mean I want him around."

"But those things you said, back at Kaplan's, I just—"

"Why are you pressing me on this?" Oliver snapped. "I thought you of all people would understand. He got your dad shot!"

"Well, yeah," Matilda conceded. "But he didn't mean to." She leaned into Oliver, nudging him with her shoulder. "I don't know, maybe I'm mellowing with age."

"You know, you said some stuff, too, that day," Oliver countered. "About him moving all of us around like chess pieces. Remember that?"

"You're right, I did."

"Then why are you defending him?"

Matilda thought for a moment. "When things were really bad, when it counted the most, he showed up. He threw himself in front of a bullet. The smartest man in the world did the dumbest thing he could possibly do. Because when you love someone, it doesn't matter how smart you are. You're always going to wind up thinking with your heart."

Matilda got up from the bleachers.

"It's up to you, Oliver," she said. "But I think someone like that deserves a second chance."

Oliver stood in the hospital hallway, watching through the door as Preston Oglethorpe slowly gathered his things. He was being discharged. Standing in the hospital room by himself, Preston looked fragile, small even. Without all his computers and chalkboards and equations, he looked completely vulnerable, like a turtle out of its shell.

Oliver tapped lightly on the open door.

"Oliver, hi," Preston said, turning a bit too quickly to face him and wincing from the pain.

"Hi," Oliver said.

"They're letting me out today," Preston said.

"Yeah. My mom said."

"How are you two doing?"

"Okay," Oliver said. "She got a job."

"Oh?"

"It means we can keep the house and we don't have to move to Massachusetts."

"That's wonderful news."

"Yeah," Oliver said. "You don't have to pretend to be surprised." The words came out more biting than Oliver had meant them. But he couldn't help feeling like it had to be said.

They were quiet for a moment, neither one sure what to say next. Then Oliver reached into his jacket pocket and pulled out a little box.

"Here," Oliver said, handing Preston the box. "It's a new watch. Seeing as how I broke your old one."

"Oh," Preston said, taking the box delicately in his hands, opening it, and peering inside. "That's very kind. Thank you."

"I need to ask you something," Oliver said directly. "All the things you planned, the stuff that you made happen and all that?"

Oliver could tell that Preston knew what he was going to ask, but the man wasn't going to take away his right to ask it.

"Did you have anything to do with my dad leaving us?"

"No, Oliver," Preston said. "I didn't."

Oliver stared at Preston for a long while. "I believe you," he said finally.

"Thank you, Oliver," Preston said solemnly. "And, for what it's worth, I didn't have anything to do with your mom's new job. She got that on her own."

"Really?"

"My equation fell apart the minute you got in the car, remember?"

"Then, how?" Oliver said.

"Just your mom being, well, your mom," Preston said in a way that sounded almost reverential.

"Wow," Oliver said. He was surprised how overcome he felt by this revelation. On the surface, it wasn't such a big deal. But at the same time, it was everything.

"You know," Preston said. "I've devoted my entire scientific career to finding and controlling that one elusive element, the one seemingly insignificant detail that would make everything in my life work out perfectly."

"The butterfly wings."

"Exactly." Preston chuckled a little. "Funny thing is, after all this time, I've come to realize that the unstable variable in all my equations is always me."

When Oliver looked at the man who was possibly the smartest person of all time, all he saw were the sad, faraway eyes of the child genius on that orientation video from the first day of school.

Ever since his talk with Matilda, Oliver had been torn about whether to come to the hospital to see Preston. In the end, it was something she hadn't said that had ultimately changed his mind. Something he was sure she'd figured out a while ago but kept to herself. Perhaps because she knew Oliver had to get there on his own. Either that or she just didn't want to sound like a pushy know-it-all.

She knew why Preston had concocted this whole crazy plan. Why he'd forced mango-chutney jam and beef jerky and lost dogs and new friendships into their lives.

It was about saying goodbye.

Oliver would never understand any of the dizzying formulas

Preston created, but he did know one thing for sure: that all of Preston Oglethorpe's great equations had always ended the same way. With Preston on the other side of the equal sign, alone.

Whether trapped in Kaplan's gilded cage or hiding from the world in janitor's overalls and a shaggy beard, Oliver was sure that Preston had never calculated a happy ending for himself. That he was always trapped in the last box on his massive flowchart. And that all the other boxes preceding it, everything that had happened since the boys first stepped into Henry's Market, had been Preston's way of saying goodbye to the world. His way of doing something special, something perfect for his friends and their kids and the people they loved, before he disappeared for good.

Trust the math, Preston had told Oliver. Because he believed it was all he had.

Oliver shook his head, got up, and made his way to the door. "You know," he said. "You really do think too much. All those equations, formulas, wall charts, whatever. Just a big waste of time, if you ask me. In the end, everything boils down to one number anyway."

"Really?" Preston said, intrigued. "What number is that?"

"Seven."

"Why seven?"

"That's when we have dinner. Don't be late."

"Daisy, Daisy, give me your answer do . . ."

"Oh, do shut up, Einstein," Marie Curie snapped.

Albert was singing off-key, Preston guessed, on purpose.

"He needs to get on with it," Albert said.

"And he will," Marie said. "But your caterwauling isn't helping matters."

Preston sat at the main terminal of his computer. With a couple of keystrokes he would wipe out all four of the talking portraits. Not just turn them off temporarily, but erase them completely.

He knew he had to do it, but he didn't think he could.

"It's the only way, Preston," Leonardo said. "You need to rejoin the world again, my boy. And that can't happen if you keep hiding in here with us."

"You're ready for this, I know you are," Marie added.

"This is getting way too sappy," Albert barked. "Pull the plug already."

Preston smiled. He looked over at the last portrait. Nicola Tesla, as usual, remained frozen in place. It was time.

"Goodbye, Albert," Preston said.

"Yeah, yeah," Albert grumbled as Preston hit the button, turning the portrait to black.

"Bet that felt good," Leonardo quipped.

"A little," Preston admitted.

"You know we'll always be with you," Marie said.

"Literally, seeing as he's memorized all our code," Leonardo said. "Take care, kid."

Preston shut down Leonardo's portrait. He looked at Marie, and she at him.

"I would say I'll miss you—" Marie said.

"—but seeing as you're just a bunch of ones and zeroes—" Preston followed.

"—it wouldn't be accurate," Marie finished, smiling. "Nevertheless, I reserve the right to be proud of you."

Preston nodded but didn't say anything for a few moments.

"I'm afraid," he said, finally.

"I know," Marie said. "But your life is waiting for you."

Preston's finger hovered delicately over the button.

"Goodbye, Marie."

Only the Tesla portrait remained. Preston waited a moment, just in case, but knew it was pointless. Nicola had said all he needed to weeks ago. Anything more than that just wasn't him. Not every goodbye gets a send-off.

Preston shut down the last portrait and then left the warehouse.

He had someplace to be.

There was a knock at the door promptly at seven. Oliver answered and led Preston to the backyard where Frankie's father was grilling burgers.

Oliver introduced Preston to Frankie's parents and to Steve Bishop and Frankie's aunt Josie. He pointed out Frankie's twin brothers, who were wildly attacking Archie over by the swing set.

"I hope it's not too much," Oliver said to Preston. "I know you're not exactly used to people."

"It's okay," Preston said, more, it seemed, to himself than to Oliver.

Matilda and her mom showed up, along with Floss, who had run out to the store to buy more ice. Matilda's dad, coming straight from work, showed up a little while later.

Oliver could tell how overwhelming it all was for Preston. But these were nice people, kind people. They were who they said they were, and Preston needed that. So did Oliver.

The barbecue went late into the night. No one wanted to leave. Preston, Floss, and Jimmy, once reunited, were inseparable the entire evening. And though Oliver was busy with Frankie and Matilda, he couldn't resist sneaking peeks at his mom and her childhood friends.

At one point, Oliver saw his mom take Preston's hand and admire the watch Oliver had given him. It wasn't anything fancy. In fact, it was very simple, no frills. Just a big hand, a little hand, and little dashes around the perimeter for the hours. It didn't have a little box for the date. It didn't even have a second hand.

And it would never . . . ever . . .

Beep.

ACKNOWLEDGMENTS

No one does it alone. At least no one I've ever met.

Thanks to my family, for their support and encouragement. And criticism. And for pretending not to notice when they catch me mumbling to myself.

Thank you to the keen and insightful Maggie Washburn for kindly taking the first draft of this book out for a spin.

Thanks to my amazing agent, Emily Mitchell, who despite living on the opposite edge of the country is still always there whenever I need her.

I remain beyond grateful to my editor, Jenne Abramowitz. Working with you makes me so much better; it shouldn't get to be this much fun.

Thanks bundles to the Scholastic family: Ellie Berger, Rachel Feld, Julia Eisler, Baily Crawford, Yaffa Jaskoll, Josh Berlowitz, Elisabeth Ferrari, Lizette Serrano, Emily Heddleson, Danielle Yadao, Alan Smagler, Elizabeth Whiting, Alexis Lunsford, Jackie Rubin, Nikki Mutch, Terribeth Smith, Roz Hilden, Chris Satterlund, Sue Flynn, Ann Marie Wong, Jana Haussmann, Shelly Romero, Abby McAden, and David Levithan. I'm blown away by your kindness and indefatigable awesomeness!

And finally, thank you, Kirsten. I'd be all talk if it wasn't for you.

NO PARENTS. NO RULES. NO CURFEW.
THINGS ARE ABOUT TO GET DANGEROUS . . .

Read on for a sneak peek at Keith Calabrese's
next thrilling adventure!

The following redacted interview is the only surviving document related to a series of highly classified events that have been dubbed informally (and somewhat amusingly) by the Senate Intelligence Committee as "The Mustang Redundancy."

Department of Justice
Federal Bureau
of Investigations

Witness Interview: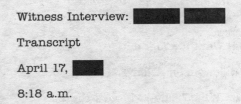

Transcript

April 17,

8:18 a.m.

[Interview of subject conducted by Special Agent Karen Hill and Special Agent Allen Dale]

[Subject, ▮▮▮▮ ▮▮▮▮, is female, 12 years of age, and will herein be referred to as "Witness 2"]

Special Agent Hill: You have to admit, it's a pretty incredible story.

Witness 2: Oh, I know. Ma'am.

Special Agent Hill: And by incredible, I'm using the "difficult to believe" definition of the term.

Witness 2: Yeah. I got that. Look, where's my brother? And where's ████?

Special Agent Hill: I believe I'm asking the questions, young lady.

Witness 2: Look, I've already told you everything. Twice. What more could you possibly need to know?

Special Agent Dale: Doughnut?

Witness 2: Huh?

Special Agent Dale: Want a doughnut?

Special Agent Hill: Seriously, Allen?

Special Agent Dale: What? The kid looks scared.

Witness 2: I'm not scared.

Special Agent Dale: I could look for one with sprinkles. Might help, like, cut the tension.

Special Agent Hill: Shut up, Allen.

Witness 2: I don't want a doughnut. I just want to see my brother and .

Special Agent Hill: Then explain to me what the three of you were doing with two known felons like ████ and ████ ████████?

Witness 2: Doing? They kidnapped us!

Special Agent Hill: I thought you said they kidnapped ███████████.

Witness 2: Well, yeah. They did. But that was before.

Special Agent Hill: At the restaurant?

Witness 2: ███ ████████, yeah.

Special Agent Hill: Where you met the ████████████ brothers?

Witness 2: No.

Special Agent Dale: Aha! Where you met ██████████████!

Witness 2: No! Like I said, we didn't meet anyone at ███ ████████. We just went there for burgers and milk-shakes. All this other stuff just sort of happened.

Special Agent Hill: See, that's where you lose me. So, the ████████████ brothers just happened to pick your car to ███ ███ ██ ███ ████ ███ ██ ███ ████ ████ ███.

Witness 2: They didn't know it was our car! They thought it was █████ ██████ car.

Special Agent Hill: To be clear, you are referring to tech billionaire █████ ████?

Witness 2: Yes! For the last time, that's the guy! Like I said, the ████████████ brothers work for him. Look, you're wasting time. You need to find him. Now.

Special Agent Hill: Take it easy.

Witness 2: No! I won't take it easy. Haven't you been listening to me at all? This guy is really dangerous. To everyone. What part of that isn't sinking into those thick skulls of yours?

Special Agent Dale: [inaudible noise, possibly a snicker]

Special Agent Hill: You know, young lady, you have a serious mouth on you. Anyone ever tell you that?

Witness 2: Once or twice. That doughnut still on the table?

Special Agent Dale: Sure. Sprinkles or jelly?

Special Agent Hill: Sit down, Allen. Okay, ███████. Let's try this again. From the beginning.

According to the United States government,

what you are about to read never happened . . .

ONE

On Friday afternoon, shortly before the final bell, Charley Decker received detention for mouthing off to her teacher. Charley didn't get in trouble much. It kind of caught everyone by surprise.

Wade was waiting for her when she finally got out. He was trying not to smirk, but he wasn't trying very hard.

"Don't start," Charley said.

"At least Mr. Bonino didn't keep you that long," Wade offered.

"He shouldn't have kept me at all," Charley protested.

Wade shrugged.

"What?"

"Charley, seriously," Wade said. "You kind of asked for it."

"What part of 'don't start' aren't you getting?"

"Fine," Wade said, dropping it. "See any familiar faces in the big house?"

"Parker Nadal was in there, too. I don't know what for."

"I do," Wade chuckled.

"Really? Who was he impersonating this time?"

"Not 'who,'" Wade corrected. "'What.' Remember the T. rex from *Jurassic Park*?"

"Sure," Charley said. "Wait. He didn't!"

"He did. During passing period. You could hear it all the way down B Hall."

"No way," Charley laughed. "Was it good?"

"Good enough to make a bunch of sixth graders cry."

"He does have a gift."

"Yeah," Wade agreed. "But hey, you mouthed off to the nicest teacher in school. Now that's hard-core."

Charley gave him a look but couldn't hold it for long. Everybody needs at least one friend who has no qualms about telling you when you're full of it. Charley had long ago realized that Wade Harris would always be that friend for her. She just wished he wasn't so good at it.

"It isn't a bad word," she huffed defiantly.

"Sure."

Charley said, "Just don't say anything in front of Greg, okay?"

"'Course," Wade said as they started walking home. "We still on, then, for New Farouk's and everything?"

"You bet," Charley said, brightening a bit. "Greg promised."

Greg was Charley's older brother. It was more than that, though. They were pals, always had been. There were five and a half years between them—Greg was eighteen and she was twelve—but he never treated her like it. He treated her more like his partner in crime. He was always there when she needed him, always had her back.

This year, though, everything was changing. Greg was a senior in high school, and soon he'd be going off to college. Charley was already starting to miss him. Greg wasn't around the house much anymore. Lately, he was always out with his friends, or at baseball practice, or with Marisa.

Mostly with Marisa.

And even when Greg was around, Marisa was usually there, too. They'd been dating all year and Greg was still totally moony for her. She even came to family game night. It was bad enough when their mom's boyfriend, Derrick, had started showing up. Now game night was practically a couples' thing. What was the point anymore?

Take two weeks ago. They were playing Scrabble—Charley, Greg, Mom, and Derrick. Marisa wasn't there, but she may as well have been because Greg was texting her, like, every two minutes. Anyway, it was Charley's turn and she had two *f*'s, an *a*, a *d*, a *t*, an *i*, and an *r*. She used them all, a natural bingo (and a double word score to boot, but who's counting), and did Greg even notice? Please, he barely looked up from his phone.

Everything was changing.

For the last week it had just been the two of them in the house. Their mom and Derrick were in Hawaii for vacation, but they'd be getting back tomorrow. At first Charley had been looking forward to this week, just her and her brother. She'd hoped it would give them a chance to hang out like they used to. But it wasn't working out that way.

One way or another, her brother always seemed to be out the door. He and Marisa had been off doing stuff together every day since Mom and Derrick left. They were always *busy*. Always on the go. Charley got to tag along sometimes, to watch Marisa's track meet, or Greg's doubleheader. Whoopee. Like that counted.

And even when Greg was around, he wasn't *there*, not really. Hanging out at home made him all twitchy and distracted. Like he was trapped, or grounded. And he barely noticed Charley anymore, even when they were in the same room together.

But tonight was going to be different. Charley was going to make sure of it. Greg had promised to take her and Wade to New

Farouk's for burgers and shakes. The diner's full name was New Farouk's Famous Ice Cream and Brazier, and they made the best milkshakes in Chicago. The burgers were good, too, but it was really all about the milkshakes. At least that's what Charley thought. It was her favorite place to eat, and the kind of hang-out thing Charley had hoped they'd be doing all week.

Then, after New Farouk's, the three of them would come back to the house and watch their favorite movies all night, just like they used to do when Greg was in middle school and Charley and Wade were just in grade school. The coolest movies. Movies they had been too young to watch. That's what made Greg such an awesome big brother. Like *Purple Rain* and the first two *Alien* movies—but you had to stop after that—and *Galaxy Quest* and *Hot Fuzz*.

Charley had the whole night planned out. Tonight was going to be like old times. Like it used to be. Tonight was going to be the best.

Wade and Charley walked through the garage on their way into Charley's house. They came in the side door and Charley dropped her bag on the kitchen island. Wade lingered behind in the doorway.

"Man," Wade said, gazing adoringly at Derrick's Mustang. "That is some car."

"You say that every time."

"It bears repeating. Every time."

Greg was upstairs; it sounded like he was on the phone.

"You still good to stay over?" Charley asked.

"No problem," Wade said as he joined her at the island. "It's a gap weekend."

Wade's parents were divorced. They were also both lawyers. They shared Wade through a joint-custody agreement that was so complicated it required a computer algorithm to enforce.

But with all the back-and-forth, there were bound to be gaps. Misread emails, blind spots in the code. Days when neither Wade's mother nor father technically had custody of Wade. But since his parents never actually talked to each other, no one really noticed.

The first time it happened, Wade hadn't said anything. He'd just gone to stay with his uncle Terry in the city and waited for someone—his parents, their lawyers, the algorithm—to figure out the mistake.

That was two years ago.

Wade didn't mind much. He always had a blast with his uncle Terry. Besides, no one had ever asked him whether he wanted a stupid computer program to tell him where to eat and sleep and do his homework. So why should he help his parents micro-manage *his* life?

Greg came downstairs. He was still in his baseball clothes, talking excitedly on his cell phone.

"No, no," he said. "I want to wait and surprise Mom and Derrick when they get back tomorrow. Yeah. Okay, see you soon." He ended the call and put the phone back in his pocket.

"Hey, you're home," he said, noticing Charley and Wade. "Where were you guys? It's later than usual."

"Loitering," Charley said.

"Light trespassing," Wade added.

"How was practice?" Charley asked, to get them off the subject.

"Aw, fine. Coach let us out early on account of yesterday's doubleheader. Never mind that, though. Guess what." His eyes looked big, like he'd just pounded two iced coffees.

"What?" Charley asked warily.

He held up his phone. "I just found out . . . I got into the University of British Columbia!"

Charley felt like somebody had just knocked the wind out of her. "In Canada?" she managed.

"Hey, that's great," Wade said, reading the acceptance email on Greg's phone. "Congratulations!"

"Thanks! It's my first choice. I'm so stoked."

Wade sat down on one of the stools while Greg gushed about how excellent UBC was going to be. Charley sat, too, but she didn't say anything. She hadn't known he was looking at schools that were thousands of miles away. She stared into space for a good ten minutes while the boys prattled on until she heard her brother say to Wade, "So, you're coming with us to New Farouk's?"

"Yeah. If that's cool."

"Absolutely," Greg said. "We need to celebrate, right?" He looked over at his sister. "Charley?"

"Huh?"

"New Farouk's? Still want to go?"

"Definitely," Charley said, perking up a little.

"Great! Let me shower and get changed. Then as soon as Marisa gets here, we'll head out."

"Great," Charley said. Then: "Wait, what?"

HOME BASE

YOUR FAVORITE BOOKS COME TO LIFE IN A BRAND-NEW DIGITAL WORLD!

- Meet your favorite characters
- Play games
- Create your own avatar
- Chat and connect with other fans
- Make your own comics
- Discover new worlds and stories
- And more!

Start your adventure today! Download the **HOME BASE** app and scan this image to unlock exclusive rewards!

SCHOLASTIC.COM/HOMEBASE

📖 **SCHOLASTIC**

HBGENERICSP